W9-DGT-279

Harlequin Presents...

KEIR DULLEA · SUSAN PENHALIGON

Leopard in the Snow

Guest Stars

KENNETH MORE · BILLIE WHITELAW

featuring GORDON THOMSON as MICHAEL
and JEREMY KEMP as BOLT

Produced by JOHN QUESTED and CHRIS HARROP
Screenplay by ANNE MATHER and JILL HYEM
Directed by GERRY O'HARA

An Anglo-Canadian Co-Production

OTHER
Harlequin Romances
by KAY THORPE

Storm Passage

by

KAY THORPE

Harlequin Books

TORONTO • LONDON • NEW YORK • AMSTERDAM • SYDNEY

Original hardcover edition published in 1977
by Mills & Boon Limited

ISBN 0-373-02109-7

Harlequin edition published October 1977

Printed in Canada

CHAPTER ONE

'MISS SMITH,' stated the Captain, 'is an exceedingly brave young woman to contemplate such a trip as this alone. I admire the spirit of adventure in the youth of today.'

'Adventure?' queried the dark-haired man seated on his left with a tilt of a brow. 'Or recklessness?'

Tara met sardonic grey eyes across the dining saloon table. 'Perhaps a bit of both,' she said coolly. 'There's an element of recklessness in any decision to get up off one's rear and see what the rest of the world has to offer. To add to the record, I'll be arriving back home eventually just about penniless too, but at least I'll have some memories to keep me going through the next few years of working for a living. Unless someone happens to leave me another legacy. Then I'd be able to see all the places I miss out on this time.'

'You have a lot of rich elderly relatives?' The satire was unconcealed.

'No,' Tara admitted, and then on an unconsciously defensive note, 'as a matter of fact, I don't have any relatives at all. This opportunity came through my godfather.' Already she was regretting having been quite so open with regard to her presence here on board the *Saratoga*, but Captain Anders had shown such a warming interest in her reasons for choosing to travel by cargo vessel in preference to the more luxurious methods that she'd really had little choice but to satisfy his curiosity. Not that she particularly minded anyone knowing her circumstances. It was only this one of her fellow passengers who had managed to make the whole venture sound so totally irresponsible. Bryant, the Captain had called him. English like herself, and yet certainly not recently domiciled there, judging from the long-standing depth of his tan. Always a person for trying to keep an open mind, she found it difficult right now with that level gaze on her. The self-assertive type, she reflected dryly. Women would have a definite place in his life, but not on the same level of existence, that was for sure! Good-looking, she supposed, if one cared for that kind of lean, hard masculinity. Her own tastes ran to a little more sensitivity and a deal less cynical worldliness.

'Personally, I agree with the Skipper,' put in the fair man in uniform seated on her right, with an air of appreciation. 'It takes nerve to come *this* far via the routes you've taken, never mind the rest. Most women would plump for a nice comfortable passenger liner if they had the choice.'

Tara smiled. 'Maybe that's the operative word. I hadn't —at least, not if I wanted to go the whole way round. I'll admit I had some qualms myself at first, but the shipping office arranged everything perfectly. I'd advise anyone considering seeing the world on a budget to use this method.' Her tone was lightly self-mocking. 'Most of my friends thought I was quite mad too.'

The First Officer grinned back. 'It's the kind of madness they'd all probably like to be capable of! How long are you planning on taking to cover the whole trip?'

'About ten weeks. I've been a couple on the way so far, though I cheated a little by taking a scheduled flight from London to Barbados. I had a three-day wait in La Guaria for my ship. It had to have a new boiler installed after one of the original ones blew up.' Blue eyes took on an added spark as they were once more drawn to the grey ones opposite. 'One of life's little setbacks. Few things go exactly according to plan. Anyway, it gave me the opportunity to see more of Venezuela than I'd hoped for.'

'And made serious inroads into your reserves of cash,' he came back shrewdly. 'Many more setbacks like that and you're going to find yourself stranded on the wrong side of the world.'

Her head came up, the light catching and streaking the heavy, honey-coloured hair. 'If that happens I wouldn't consider myself stranded, Mr Bryant. I'd get a job and make my passage money home.'

'Just like that?' His voice mocked. 'You make it sound almost plausible! Why not admit you didn't make any allowance for contingencies? No one's going to think any the worse of you.'

The irony registered but she refused to let it show. 'Let's just say I don't cross my bridges before I come to them. My passage is already paid as far as the Society Islands. After that I plan to make my way down to Tonga, and then from there across to Australia where I can stay with friends.'

'Missing out New Zealand? What a pity!'

'I'll do that next time round.' He was beginning to get to her and she didn't like it. She had to forcibly restrain herself from sharp rejoinder. That was probably what he was hoping for. His kind would gain great entertainment from nudging the lesser controlled into losing it altogether. Only he wasn't going to succeed with her. She could give as good as she got—sometimes better!

She turned her attention towards the remaining two passengers with a look of bright inquiry. 'You're both getting off in Tahiti too, aren't you?'

The elder of the pair answered for them both, dwelling smilingly on her finely boned features. 'My brother and I hope to settle in the islands. We're both of us retired, and bachelors, so we can afford to take the risk in changing our life style. Unlike yourself, we neither of us had the courage to take off for parts unknown when we were younger.'

Tara said softly, 'I think it must take a great deal more to do it now. I hope you find what you're looking for.'

'If we don't,' put in the younger brother on a jocular

note, 'it certainly won't be for want of trying!'

The Number One had moved his chair closer on the pretext of pouring her more of the excellent wine ordered by the Captain in honour of their first night out of Panama, ignoring the presence of the steward.

'Is Smith your real name?' he queried. 'Or a nom-de-plume?'

'It's real,' she said with resignation.

'And what about the other one?'

'That's real too.' She felt his glance and tilted her lips. 'Tara. My parents rather overdid the compensation.'

'I don't think so. It suits you.' He tried the name softly over, his eyes on her face with a knowing expression. 'Unusual, to say the least. I'm Mike, by the way.'

First Officer Michael Chandris, Tara decided at that moment, was a man to watch oneself with. The give an inch, take a yard type if ever she'd met one! But fun to be with in certain circumstances, no doubt, providing those same circumstances precluded the possibility of being left alone with him. The other officers present at the table were watching the two of them with varying expressions. Their senior's prowess with members of the fair sex was probably shipboard legend. A little abruptly she turned back to the Captain at the head of the long table.

'Your offices said you would be able to fix me up with a passage onwards from Tahiti, Captain. Is that right?'

'I'm sure of it—although it won't be with this same line. There are plenty of island steamers with cabin room. They'll get you there eventually via a few ports of call on the way.'

'Do we make any calls ourselves apart from Cocos Island?'

'One scheduled one to drop off our friend here,' indicating the man at his other side. 'Mr Bryant owns the island of Mataleta.'

'Owns?' Involuntarily her eyes widened as they flashed a glance at her opposite partner. She caught the faint twist of his lips and bit her own. All right, so she was impressed. Who wouldn't be? To actually own a Pacific island was surely the stuff dreams were made of. But he needn't think she was going to start fawning round him because of it. Rich or poor, the man retained the same insufferable qualities. 'Fascinating,' she said. 'Did your ancestors take it?'

'No,' he returned without particular inflection. 'My great-great-grandfather was given it for services rendered. It once formed the outer limits of the Marquesas group. I share it now with a partner.'

'How is he?' The Captain's tone had altered, taken on a deeper underlying note.

The other man shrugged, face impassive. 'As well as can be expected. The progression is slow. That's what makes it worse for him in a way. He could live for years while gradually losing his faculties.'

'And nothing can be done to arrest it?'

'Nothing.' It was said flatly.

Obviously feeling it was time to change the subject, Captain Anders commented, 'That daughter of yours must be growing up fast. How old will she be now?'

'Nine.' The flatness was still there, but his expression had subtly altered. His eyes came back to Tara, flicking over her hair and face with a hint of contempt. 'Time she was going away to school. The last governess only stayed two months.'

The older man chuckled. 'No stamina, that's the trouble. You should get married again, Nick.' He seemed to catch himself up, looked suddenly uncomfortable. 'Well, maybe school's the best idea.'

A widower? Tara found herself wondering. Or divorced? Odd, but she couldn't imagine him ever having been a married man at all. What kind of woman would take on such a formidable partner? Unless it was the marriage itself that had soured him. She stole another glance at the ruthless line of his mouth and felt a quiver run through her. No, that look was bred in him. He'd go his own way regardless of anyone or anything. A man to steer well clear of—but then she wasn't a woman in love.

It was late when they finished dinner. Tara excused herself on the grounds of unpacking still to do and went aft to her cabin on the same deck. Accommodation aboard the *Saratoga* wasn't over-spacious, but for what she was paying there was small room for complaint. There was a second berth above her own—empty this trip, of course, she being the only female passenger. Three cabins were given over to human freight, she knew. Nick Bryant had the one next door to this, which meant that the Regan brothers were sharing the other on the far side. They must be terribly cramped, but she doubted if they minded. They had waited most of their lives to make this trip. She was fortunate enough to be making hers closer to the beginning.

News of the legacy had come just before her twenty-second birthday, all the more unexpected because she hadn't even seen her godfather in years. Life hadn't been all that easy since her father had died eighteen months ago. She supposed she could have done the sensible thing and invested the money; that was what everyone had advised her to do. But look what she would have missed already: the unbelievable warmth and beauty of the Caribbean islands; the excitement of port-hopping along the Venezuelan and Columbian coasts; the thrill of the Panama Canal and emergence on the other side of a continent. No, she regretted none of it. Time enough to think about the future when all this was over. For the present, she had another two months of voyaging ahead of her, and she was going to make the most of them.

She was still stowing away items from her compact wardrobe when the knock came on the door. When she went to open it Mike Chandris stood there.

'Thought you might like to be shown round the ship,' he offered. His smile was suggestive. 'There's a regular old Pacific moon up there tonight.'

'The same one we have back home, I think, unless they've duplicated that too.' Tara smiled back without moving. 'I'll give it a miss this time. It's been a bit of a hectic day. Thanks for the thought, anyway.'

'Oh, come on,' he coaxed, refusing to give in that easily. 'You can't be so tired at your age. It's a calm sea. We might not get it like this again for some time, according to the weather forecast. There's a force nine scheduled for tomorrow forenoon.'

Tara suppressed her immediate reactions. Gales weren't rare at sea. The *Saratoga* would have weathered worse. 'Then we all ought to be getting our sleep while we can,' she said. 'Didn't you say your watch began at four a.m.?'

'Yes. One reason why I'd welcome a little light relief first.' He was still reluctant to accept the refusal. 'We've a couple of weeks to kill before we reach the Societies. You're not going to stay aloof all the time, I hope.'

'It depends on how friendly you're counting on getting,' she returned frankly. 'I realise being the only female on board makes me a novelty, but I'm only here for the ride, Mike.'

This time his grin was spontaneous. 'That's another thing I like about you. You're not devious.'

'Don't count on it. There's ...' She broke off as Nick Bryant passed along the narrow alleyway, her face warming under the brief glance he tossed her over Mike's shoulder. 'I think it's time you went,' she added low-toned to the latter. 'Goodnight.'

She could hear movement from next door as she prepared for bed; the running of water into the small hand-basin tucked away into a corner of the cabin. By the time she was tucked up in her own berth the sounds had stopped and silence reigned, apart from the incessant creaking and groanings which pervaded every ship. Right now the motion was regular and pleasant, like being lulled to sleep in a rocking chair. So far her voyages had been along the coast, thereby avoiding any real variations of weather, but that was a matter soon to be rectified, according to what Mike Chandris had said. The Pacific was immense and they were heading right out into the middle of it. Anything could happen. But wasn't that a part of the reason she was here? Uncertainty, apprehension—they were both necessary elements to adventure. And what an adventure! The kind most people her age would give their eye teeth to experience. To see the world at twenty-two, or as much of it as she could manage, at any rate. It might lack practicality, but what of it? Life was meant to be lived, not saved for.

Someone was shaking her gently, urging her to wake up. She opened her eyes to find the cabin light on and Nick Bryant bending over her, face shadowed by his own bulk, fingers strong and warm on her bare shoulder.

'Don't scream,' he said with a mocking inflection. 'You were having a nightmare—calling out in your sleep. I thought I'd better come in and waken you before you woke the whole ship.'

Tara registered the dampness of perspiration on her skin, the rapid beating of her heart, and wondered how much of it was due to nightmare and how much to the shock of finding this man here in her cabin. She moved abruptly, shrugging off his hand and pulling the blanket closer about her as she came up on one elbow. 'I don't have any recollection of dreaming,' she said.

'Well, you were. Very vividly, from the way you were throwing yourself about.' He made no attempt to move away from the berth. 'I'd have said you were fighting with

12

something—or someone.' The pause held deliberation. 'Premonition, maybe. The way you're carrying on it could easily happen.'

'Carrying on?' She said it tautly. 'I'm not sure what that's supposed to mean.'

'It means that your subconscious could be trying to tell you what common sense should already have warned you about.' He stuck his hands in the pockets of his dark silk dressing gown, surveying her with calculated appraisal. 'Have you any notion at all of what you're asking for travelling about on your own like this? Chandris can't be the first to react that way.'

Tara looked back at him without flinching. 'What way?'

'Don't try acting dense. He was quick enough to follow through. A man of his kind has little finesse.'

'I suppose you should know.' She saw his face darken and knew a momentary trepidation, but it was too late now to retract. 'Does it really have anything to do with you anyway?' she tagged on with a lift of her chin. 'I can cope with Mike Chandris.'

'Can you? I wonder.' The mockery had gone from his voice; it was edged now with something else. 'Perhaps I should leave you to do it. You might learn something from the experience.'

'Fine.' Her own voice bit. 'The door's over there.'

He remained where he was, eyes narrowed dangerously, mouth a taut line. 'Did anybody ever spank you?' he said. 'Good and hard!'

'Not since I was eight.' She was angry but in control of herself. 'I'm a wee bit past it now.'

'You're probably right.' The glint increased as he bent and pushed her back into the pillow. 'But you're not past this.'

With his mouth on hers and his hands holding her down, Tara found it impossible to do anything but accept retribution. The kiss bruised her, yet it also stirred a deep down measure of response she could not entirely control. That he too had recognised it was evidenced by the look on his face when he at last raised his head from hers.

'So you can cope,' he said tauntingly. 'And I wasn't even trying. Still think you're capable of holding off any comers?'

'They wouldn't get this far,' she responded with an effort. 'In future I'll make sure my door is locked—to everybody!'

'That's about the wisest thing you've said since we met.' He got to his feet again, looming over her with a smile on his lips she longed to wipe off. 'Don't fret. You'll learn how to spit in a man's eye one of these fine days.'

'I hope ...' her voice quivered a little with the need to hurt ... 'somebody once spat in *your* eye!'

His laugh was brittle. 'I'm sure you do. Sleep tight. I'll be right next door.'

She lay still until the door had closed behind him, only then putting up a hand to touch her lips where the imprint still lingered. A few brief hours ago she hadn't even known Nick Bryant existed, and now ...

To say she hated him would be childish—and untrue. The emotions he aroused in her were nowhere near so easily defined. From the moment of meeting there had been some element present between them; a spark waiting to be ignited. It hadn't been her he had been kissing just then, it had been someone else; someone he had wanted to hurt— perhaps even someone she reminded him of. Odd how it stung to know that. Suddenly and desperately she wished herself anywhere but on the *Saratoga*. This whole trip had started to go sour.

CHAPTER TWO

THE wind was already rising fast by daybreak. Tired after a restless night, Tara gave breakfast a miss and stayed on in her berth for a while, until the steep pitching of the ship forced her to abandon it. Lying down made it worse. At least on her feet she felt better able to cope with the see-sawing movement.

It was cool on deck, the sea a heavily rolling grey beneath a sky overcast and dull—not the Pacific she had anticipated, but there was plenty of time yet. This mightn't last long. By tonight it would most likely have blown itself out. Meanwhile, she must be grateful that she appeared to have found her sea-legs all right. Being ill would really have put the damper on the whole project.

In the light of day last night seemed like a bad dream, except that she knew it wasn't. Nick Bryant was still right here on the ship, and would be for several days. No doubt her missing breakfast would have given him cause for amusement. He was certain to think he was the reason.

If she were honest with herself, he was a great part of it. The thought of facing that cynical gaze across the table had been more than she could contemplate. On the other hand, she was going to have to face him again some time. She couldn't stay in her cabin for the whole voyage. By lunch-time she had to have regained enough of her equilibrium to be able to walk into the saloon with apparent unconcern. Whatever his motives, all he'd done was kiss her, and it wasn't exactly the first time she'd been kissed. Put it down to experience and learn from it.

'Not a very good morning, is it?' The elder of the two

15

Regan brothers joined her at the rail, looking out at the heaving seas with a wry grimace. 'And it's going to get worse before it gets better, I understand. We're running into a storm.'

Tara glanced at him quickly. 'We're not attempting to go round it?'

'I shouldn't imagine so. The ship has to be in Tahiti by a week on Tuesday in order to pick up cargo. A day's delay can cost the company a great deal of money.' He added reassuringly, 'I'm sure there's nothing to worry about. The _Saratoga_ is a well-weathered ship. Captain Anders tells me she survived a hurricane in the Caribbean a couple of years back—came right through it with only a couple of sprung plates and a little superstructural damage. The Met report last night forecast moderate to severe for the whole area, so we might miss the worst of it anyway.'

'What about this morning's forecast?'

'I'm not sure. They're having a bit of trouble with the radio. Nothing they can't put right in a couple of hours, I'm told.' He gave her a quick appraising look. 'We missed you at breakfast. That young Third Officer wanted to have some sent along to your cabin, but Bryant said you'd rather be left alone. Feeling a bit off-colour, were you?'

'A bit.' Tara was inwardly fuming but couldn't afford to let it show. 'I rarely eat breakfast at home. Just a cup of coffee usually, perhaps a slice of toast when I have the time.'

'It's a mistake. You'll rue it later on in life, believe me.' He smiled suddenly. 'Typical of the old to preach to the young, isn't it?'

Tara laughed, studying the kindly features beneath the iron-grey hair. 'You can't be as old as you try to make yourself sound, retired or not.'

'I could be your grandfather.' His eyes twinkled back. 'As a matter of fact, the retirement was voluntary. We sold up our business interests in order to do what we're doing now.

One advantage of not having families to care for.'

There was a note in his voice which belied the lightness of the statement. Tara said impulsively, 'You've never felt the need for a family of your own?'

'Never found the time.' This time the tone was definitely rueful. 'Work becomes a way of life. You put things off for so long, then one day you wake up and find it's too late.'

'But not for this, or you wouldn't be here now.'

'No, not for this.' He paused, cleared his throat, then said on a different note, 'Look, I know you'll think I'm an interfering old fool, but what Bryant was saying last night made some sense. You're young, and very attractive, and entirely unprotected. Like the Captain, I admire your spirit, but unlike him I can see the dangers. So far you've been fortunate—and you're certainly safe enough while you're aboard the *Saratoga*—only what about the rest of your tour? Those island steamers might be cheap; they'll also be far from choosy about the kind of people they carry.'

Not this again! Tara thought resignedly. Aloud she said, 'It's good of you to bother about me, Mr Regan, but I honestly have thought about all that. If I hadn't been prepared to take a few risks I'd never have come on this trip in the first place. I'll be careful. That's all I can do.'

'But not all *I* can do.' He went on quickly before she could interrupt. 'I'd like to be allowed to put you on a plane from Tahiti straight through to your friends in Australia, if I may. You'd miss Tonga, but it's only one island. Will you let me do that—for my own peace of mind, at least?'

She hesitated before replying, aware of his sincerity and reluctant to say anything that might seem ungrateful. 'You're very kind,' she managed at last. 'And please don't think I don't appreciate it, only I have to do it my own way and out of my own pocket.'

'Pride?' he suggested on a deprecatory note.

'If you like.' She gave him an oblique glance. 'What

17

would you call accepting money from a stranger?'

'Not money, just a plane ticket.'

'That's splitting hairs.' She made a small impatient movement. 'I wish someone would credit me with enough sense to look out for myself. Men take this protection thing too far!' She saw his chagrined expression and caught herself up in quick self-criticism. 'I'm sorry, I didn't mean it to sound quite like that. But you must see how impossible it is for me to accept your offer, well-meant though it obviously was. Even if I could promise to return the money after I get back I couldn't take it. Don't you see, it just wouldn't be the same.'

He sighed. 'I understand perfectly. It won't stop me worrying about you after you leave Tahiti.'

It was time to change the subject. Tara did so before he could say anything else. 'Is your brother not as good a sailor as you?'

'Wes? Oh, he's all right. He's down below with his stamp collection. Nothing would persuade him to leave that behind.' The wryly humorous note was back. 'Another compensation, you might say.' His glance went beyond her and altered a little. 'Hardly tropical weather, is it?'

Tara had stiffened instinctively even before the reply came. She didn't turn her head as Nick Bryant moved up on her other side.

'It's a bad time of year,' he said. 'We'll survive.' He paused and she could feel his eyes on her. 'Feeling better?'

'I was never ill,' she came back. 'Just tired. I had a broken night.'

'Didn't we all!' The comment was light. 'There'll be coffee in the saloon about now, if you're interested.'

'You've sailed with the *Saratoga* before?' asked the older man.

'Any number of times. She's the main supply ship for Mataleta when she's on this run.'

'You mean you can only leave or return to the island via the cargo ships?'

'Not exactly. There's a fairly regular inter-island boat schedule. This trip I preferred to use the *Saratoga* both ways.'

'You've been away some time, then?'

'Two months.' There was something in his tone which discouraged further interest. 'Come and have that coffee while it's still hot. The Captain will probably join us if he's not required on the bridge.'

Tara went because it was easier than refusing. Anyway, she was more than ready for a hot drink. The swell had grown heavier even while they had been standing up there. Entering the ship through the watertight door while Gerald Regan held it back for her, she almost fell as the deck canted to a particularly steep angle, felt a hand come hard under her elbow and was urged up and forward with a firmness nothing could resist.

It was good to be inside out of the wind, comparatively sheltered though they'd been by the bridge superstructure. She disengaged herself from the supporting hand by pressing ahead towards the companionway down to the lower deck, clutching the handrail as the ship lurched again.

'Don't try to run before you can walk,' Nick Bryant advised, sounding impatient. 'You'll be finishing your tour quicker than you anticipate if you break a limb falling down there.'

'I've no intention of falling down anywhere,' she retorted coolly. 'If anything, my reactions are probably quicker than yours!'

'Want to put it to the test?' It was said for her ears only on a note which brought a warmth to her cheeks. 'Ten to one says you'd lose, but if you want to take the risk again ...'

The other man had dropped back owing to the narrowness of the alleyway. Tara was thankful he could not overhear. She was out of her depth with this man and he knew it. She wished to heaven she had left well alone.

Captain Anders already half filled the small saloon, coffee mug tipping dangerously as he emphasised some point to Wesley Regan with expansive gestures. He saw them comfortably seated and provided with coffee, then despatched the steward to refill the pot in the galley.

'Going to be a pretty rough night, I'm afraid,' he announced with a reassuring lack of concern. 'Should be through the worst of it by this time tomorrow, though. Sorry we don't have time to run round it. Fuel wouldn't allow for that anyway—too extensive.' He looked across at Tara. 'Think you'll be able to take it, Miss Smith?'

Him too! She refused to meet Nick Bryant's satirical gaze. 'If I said no, would you be likely to turn back?' she asked on as light a note as she could manage.

The Captain of the *Saratoga* laughed and shook his head. 'No chance. Nothing short of a typhoon could make me consider that. I must say you seem to be adjusting well enough. Not exactly the stablest of ships is the *Saratoga*. Too broad in the beam.'

'A common female failing,' Gerald Regan agreed, then smiled in Tara's direction. 'Present company excepted, of course. Only the younger element should wear trousers.'

Tara grinned back. 'They're not trousers, they're jeans. There's a subtle difference.'

'So one observes.'

The arrival of the Chief Engineer brought conversation to a general halt as a reshuffle took place to find him a seat. Nick Bryant settled matters finally by getting up and perching on the arm of Tara's chair, waving aside the protests of the newcomer.

'I've been here too often to need any cosseting,' he said easily. 'Sit down, man.'

Discussion broke out again as Wesley Regan put a question to the Chief about the speed of the ship in the conditions prevailing. Tara listened with half an ear, all too vitally aware of the arm almost rubbing hers, of the denim-clad legs casually crossed so that one foot jutted, as if to bar her from leaving the seat. Like herself, he wore a sweater—cashmere, if she weren't mistaken—the creamy whiteness emphasising the darkness of his hair. There was a faint elusive scent of aftershave, purely male in its connotations. It would be, of course. Everything about him was vibrantly male—especially his attitudes. It was useless denying his attraction. Few women could remain undisturbed by the proximity of a man as used as this one obviously was to getting his own way. Something to do with ancestry, she supposed. She wondered how old he was. Thirty-three or four, perhaps. Almost certainly no more than that, despite his assurance. She wished desperately that he would move.

'Stop detesting me quite so hard,' he said on a low note of amusement. 'I can feel the vibrations from here.'

Tara didn't bother trying to deny it. What was the use? 'You must be accustomed to dislike,' she retorted in the same low tones. 'Why let it bother you?'

'I didn't say it bothered me.' There was a pause and his voice took on a new note. 'Are you scared of storms?'

'Not unduly.' She looked up at him for a moment. 'Why?'

He shrugged. 'You looked perturbed when Dan was talking about rough weather. He noticed it too. It won't be a very comfortable ride, but we're not likely to run into any real trouble. Do you know how to use a lifejacket?'

'No,' she admitted. 'Thanks for the reassurance!'

'It's standard safety procedure—or should be if Dan ever got round to it. There's one stowed in your cabin. We'll go along after you've finished your coffee and I'll show you how to put it on. Our lifeboat station is number three, and you're supposed to know the quickest route there from your cabin.'

'I'll find it.' Her tone was short. 'I daresay I can fathom out the lifejacket for myself too, thanks.'

'Not good enough. They're awkward items. I said I'd show you and I will.' He sounded intolerant again. 'Like it or not, you're going to have to learn to accept dependence on others while you're aboard this ship. A lone female is liability enough without making things worse by being pigheaded about it.'

Tara said no more. There seemed little point. They left the salon at the same time as Dan Anders, took their leave of him at the foot of the companionway leading up to the bridge housing and proceeded along the alleyway to her cabin. Nick found the lifejacket packed away on a top shelf of the locker along with another for the spare berth. He straightened out the tapes and bade her slip her arms into the holes provided, then showed her how to fasten the toggle and cross both tapes behind her back before tying them in front at waist level. There was a whistle in its own little pocket, and a battery-charged signal light activated automatically by contact with sea water.

Tara could have sorted it out for herself, she was certain, with a little trouble, but it seemed policy not to say so. 'Thanks,' she said instead.

'No trouble.' He watched her take off the jacket and stow it safely back in its allotted place before going on, 'The quickest way to your boat station is via the companionway we came down from the deck by. Boat three is almost directly opposite. Any questions?'

'No.' She was hard put to keep any trace of irony from her voice. 'You seem to have covered just about everything.'

'Don't let it get you down.' He went to the door. 'See you at lunch.'

Tara wondered if he would. The steadily increasing roll

of the ship was beginning to take effect in a far from pleasant manner. That coffee hadn't been a good idea, she decided, feeling the perspiration bead her upper lip—not on an empty stomach. She was going to have to lie down for a while until the nausea eased.

She was still lying in the berth with no idea of how much time had passed when the knock came on the door. Nick put his head round it in answer to her weak invitation, took one look at her and nodded judiciously. 'I thought that might be it. You were fighting it earlier. Stay where you are, I'll be back in a minute.'

She was hardly going anywhere feeling like this, she thought peevishly as he vanished again. And the last person she wanted round her was him! She closed her eyes and turned her face to the bulkhead, hoping he would think her asleep when he did come back. Whatever remedy he might be bringing she didn't want it. She didn't want anything but to be left alone to die.

When the door opened again she made no movement, but he wasn't deceived. He came across to the berth, sitting down on the edge of the mattress to extend a palm holding a couple of tablets.

'Take these first. No water. That wouldn't rest easy.'

She took them from him because there seemed little choice, slipping them into her mouth and swallowing dryly, then burrowing her face back into the pillow with a faint moan. 'Just leave me alone, will you, please?' she muttered between teeth clenched against the waves of nausea.

'Not yet. You're going to eat some of these biscuits. Half the trouble is having nothing on your stomach.'

'I can't.'

'You can.' Gently but inexorably he turned her over towards him. 'Try and sit up a bit or you'll choke on the crumbs. There's a plateful of digestives. Just keep right on nibbling them. It's the best remedy of all. The tablets will

23

take care of the balance adjustment. Come on,' as she still resisted. 'You'll feel better, I promise.'

'Why should you care *how* I feel?' She was being childish, and she knew it, but it didn't seem to make any difference. 'I'm not your responsibility!'

'Call it the Good Samaritan in me. I wouldn't leave a sick cat to fend for itself.' He held out the plate of biscuits. 'Eat.'

The first one took some getting down, and made no appreciable impact on her condition. She tried to refuse a second, but he wouldn't let her. The third was easier, the nausea already beginning to pass a little by the time she had finished it. In all she took four, and then could eat no more. Nick made no further attempt to persuade her.

'I'd try and sleep now,' he said, getting back to his feet again. 'There's an adequate supply of pills in the medicine chest so you can have another dose in three or four hours if you still need it. With any luck you might even make dinner.' He paused, looking down at her. 'Want me to lock your door from the outside so you don't get disturbed? You only have to pull the lever down again if you wanted to get out.'

Tara nodded, not trusting herself to speak. She waited until he was almost at the door before saying in a small voice, 'Sorry I was such a baby over this. I never could bear being ill.'

'We're none of us supplied with all the fortitude we'd like.' For the first time his smile, though faint, was lacking in mockery. 'Think nothing of it. You'll be fighting fit again by this time tomorrow.'

She must have slept almost immediately, for when she opened her eyes again the cabin was in darkness, with only the faintly lighter grey circle of the port outlined in it. There were no stars, she realised, and the motion of the ship was distinctly worse than it had been earlier. Surprisingly, she felt no ill effects when she lifted her head to switch on the light.

Her watch said seven-fifteen. That meant she must have slept for almost six hours! Probably the pills. She wasn't used to taking drugs in any shape or form. Dinner wasn't until eight-thirty. Plenty of time to take a shower and get into some fresh clothes. Sleeping in these hadn't exactly enhanced them.

For the first time she realised that she was partially covered by a blanket, yet she was certain it had not been there when she went to sleep. Someone must have been in while she slept. The steward, perhaps? But he would hardly be likely to have lingered long enough to do this once he'd realised she was in the berth. That left Nick Bryant. He was the only other person who had a key to the cabin. The knowledge brought a mixed reaction. There seemed so many different sides to the man's nature. If he hadn't bullied her into taking those biscuits this afternoon she would very likely have still been feeling rotten—yet last night his bullying had been of a very different sort. One could only hope that his better instincts would continue to prevail.

She got to and from the bathroom without meeting anyone, keeping her feet by bracing herself against the bulkheads with her hands. Dressing was a matter of timing, especially when it came to pulling on a pair of tights. It took even longer to apply a light make-up, but at last she was ready to go, neat and slender in the tan cotton which was one of only three dresses she had brought with her. Nonirons were a boon on a trip like this. Strung up over the cabin basin, they'd drip merrily all night and be dry again ready to wear by morning. The *Saratoga* had a laundry for the crew, of course, and she'd been told to give the steward anything she needed washing while she was on board. It made life that little bit easier.

25

The knock on the door brought a surge of some emotion she couldn't quite define—or didn't want to define. It was almost a relief to find the First Officer standing there when she opened it.

'Thought I wasn't going to get to see you again,' he said. 'How do you feel?'

'Like a new person,' she said, and saw his lips widen.

'I'm glad you're not. I was pretty well satisfied with the old one. Ready to eat?'

She nodded and went out to join him, pulling the door to behind her and reminding herself to ask Nick Bryant for the key.

'Have you been on watch?' she asked as they made their way along the tilting alleyway.

'Just come off about fifteen minutes ago. Had to do a quick reshuffle, I can tell you, to get spruced up in time to come and collect you.'

'I'm flattered,' she said lightly. 'There was a time when I thought I wouldn't make it myself. If it . . .'

'Steady!' He shot an arm about her waist as the deck canted sharply to starboard and seemed to linger there for interminable seconds, bracing her against him. 'Just lean on me.'

For the moment there was no alternative, yet there was something in the way he held her that kept Tara from relaxing. She supposed it had been inevitable that Nick Bryant should choose to emerge from his cabin before she could right herself again. She pressed herself away from the Number One as the ship came slowly back on to an even keel, meeting the grey eyes with a sinking sensation deep down inside.

'Glad to see you're feeling yourself again,' he commented.

They entered the dining saloon all together, to find the Regans already there and seated, along with those of the officers not on watch. The Captain was missing, and sent his apologies. The fact that he deemed his presence on the bridge at this hour more essential gave rise to the kind of speculation Tara felt was better ignored.

It was not a comfortable meal, and not entirely due to the rolling of the ship. With Mike Chandris at her side and Nick opposite, she felt between the devil and the deep blue sea. She was thankful to concentrate most of her attention on Gerald Regan, who was discussing Tahitian history with the Chief Engineer.

Afterwards in the for'ard saloon, it was the Number One who occupied the arm of Tara's chair, using the motion of the ship as an excuse to slide a supporting arm along the back of it behind her head where she could feel it whenever she moved. The storm was the main topic of conversation. They were going to miss the centre of it, Mike Chandris had said over dinner, but it was likely to stay rough at least overnight. By his reckoning they should have run through to clear weather by mid-morning.

The tannoy request for him to report to the bridge brought a grimace of disgust but no particular surprise. 'The Third's next to useless outside a swimming pool,' he commented uncharitably. 'Needs a computer to tell him left from right!'

The Chief Engineer heaved himself to his feet as his fellow officer left, expression revealing little. 'About time I paid a visit below myself. 'Night, everybody.'

Nobody really wanted to retire this early, but there was little to stay up for. Wesley Regan was looking distinctly off-colour, Tara noted, though obviously trying his best to fight it off. The knowledge awoke a faint sense of queasiness in her again, and she swallowed, dreading a return of the afternoon's malaise.

'I've still got your key in my cabin,' Nick said as they left the saloon. 'Need any more pills?'

She tried to say it casually, unwilling to admit to any

further weakness. 'It might not be a bad idea to have some handy.'

'I'll give you a couple of doses. Two now, two more if you happen to wake in the early hours.'

She cast him a glance, clutching the handrail to stop herself from stumbling into him as they moved. 'Do you carry your own supply?'

'No, I took the precaution of asking for some to be brought down just in case.'

She considered that before asking, 'Why not directly to my cabin, if I was the "in case" you had in mind?'

'Policy. You might have felt moved to throw the things in the steward's face.'

But not in his, she conjectured from his tone. Well, he was right about that at least.

She stayed in the doorway of her own cabin while he fetched the key and tablets, aware of cool contempt in his attitude but unable to do much about it. If he thought her receptive to Mike Chandris's attentions he would have to go right on thinking so, because nothing was going to make her try explaining away that scene in the alleyway earlier. He had come to her aid that afternoon, it was true, but that gave him no right of censure, called for *or* uncalled for.

'Thanks for all your help,' she said stiffly when he came back with the things. 'I'm grateful.'

His nod was indifferent. 'You're welcome. Goodnight.'

The explosion came as Tara was turning into the cabin, the deck lifting beneath her feet with a violence which catapulted her backwards across the alleyway to land in a stunned heap against the bulkhead. She didn't lose consciousness, but it was a moment or two before she could gather her senses enough to push herself upright. There was noise everywhere, loud and continuous; hooters blasting, men shouting, the roar of escaping steam somewhere deep in the bowels of the ship. Dazedly she registered the crazy

28

tilt of the deck from where she knelt, felt the sickening vibrations running the whole length of the vessel.

Fear swept in on her, cancelling out the pain from her bruises as she tried to scramble to her feet. Then Nick was there, hands under her armpits as he hauled her upright, face a taut mask beneath the stream of blood coming from a gash over his left temple.

'Your head,' she said stupidly. 'You've cut your head.'

'It's nothing.' His voice was urgent. 'Are you all right?'

Her nod was uncertain. 'What happened?'

'We hit something.' Even as he spoke he was pushing her towards her cabin. 'Get your lifebelt and put it on. Now!'

He was back with his own before she had even got the locker open, fetching it out and putting her into it before bothering about himself. The deck had not yet righted itself, listing to starboard with a definite downward tilt towards the bows. Outside the cacophony of sound continued, overlaid by running feet and the groaning of strained metal.

'Come on,' Nick commanded, and then took her by the arm when she didn't move, urging her towards the door.

'Where to?' she said on a rising note of panic, and attempted to turn back into the cabin. 'My handbag. I haven't got my handbag!'

'Leave it. You can get it later.' He refused to let her go. 'That's lifeboat stations they're sounding, you little fool!'

Lifeboat stations! Terror gripped her. That meant they were abandoning ship! But it couldn't be, could it? It was only bare minutes since the explosion. A ship didn't sink in minutes!

'Cross your bridges when you come to them, remember?' Somehow they were outside in the alleyway, hurrying aft with the Regans close on their heels. Nick still held her in the same inexorable grip, but she felt nothing. It was another nightmare. It had to be a nightmare! This couldn't possibly be happening in reality.

The blast of wind and rain full in her face carried all the conviction she needed. Number three boat was already slung out on its davits and lowered to the bay, dangling there jerkily as the ship lurched, the men already in it hanging on to the ropes. Tara found herself lifted bodily and slung over the gunwale on to hard boards, saw Nick standing there on the deck looking towards the stern with his hands cupped about his mouth as if he were trying to make himself heard above the noise of the wind. Then sudden darkness swept over her and she knew no more.

CHAPTER THREE

SHE came to slowly and reluctantly, as if her mind, even in unconsciousness, knew what waited. The wind still howled, the night was black as pitch, but the immediate world had shrunk to the size of the boat in which she lay. A man was bending over her, features indistinguishable in the rain-lashed darkness. She knew it was Nick only by his touch; by the tensile strength of the hand supporting her neck. Beyond him she could see the terrifying heave of foam-crested waves, feel the boat rise like a funicular car up the side of another to slide sickeningly over the lip and down again into a bottomless trough.

'Don't move,' Nick said close to her ear. 'You may have concussion. Can you see clearly?'

'I can see you.' It wasn't quite true, but his closeness was comforting. Her voice sounded odd. She swallowed, felt something pop in her ears and tried again, her lips close to the lean wet face. 'Wh-what happened to the ship?'

'She's gone.' The statement was flat. 'Went down like a stone. We think everyone got away.'

'But how ... why?' It was difficult to talk in these conditions, but she couldn't accept what she was hearing. 'There was an explosion, I remember, but what ...'

'We hit a mine—an old one probably left over from the war. At least, that's what's assumed. It tore the bows out below the waterline, flooded the forward holds in minutes. She didn't stand a chance.' He was giving it to her without any frills, as if he knew that was how she would want it. No going back; the *Saratoga* no longer existed. They were on their own.

31

'Man in the water!' The shout reached them even above the elements. Two of the boat's other occupants were leaning out on the starboard side with an oar stretched, fishing desperately for the lifejacketed form with its tiny flashing light. Whoever it was he was still alive, for a triumphant cry went up as contact was made. A moment later the man was being hauled over the side, water streaming from his sodden uniform, the inflated lifebelt still beaming its signal.

Nick left Tara for a moment or two to see who the man was, returning to say briefly, 'It's Chandris. He'll be all right. That makes us a round dozen. Does your head hurt?'

'It aches. Not too badly.' She was lying in the stern of the boat with something soft under her head. Spray soaked them both along with the rain. Some of the men were already bailing. No chance to get the canvas cover up in this weather. They would just have to wait till it eased – if it ever did. In the meantime they could only hope, and pray, for the night to pass.

The rain stopped first, bringing some slight relief. Towards two o'clock the wind began dropping appreciably, although the seas stayed high. Despite the discomfort of wet clothing and low temperatures, Tara slept eventually, too exhausted for even fear to hold any further sway.

When she opened her eyes again it was daylight, the sky clear and blue above, the motion of the boat almost pleasant compared with that of the night before. Nick was some distance away with his back to her, sitting on one of the thwarts with a couple of the other men in some kind of conference. The pale fawn suit was creased and wrinkled in the sunlight, except where the jacket stretched across broad shoulders. His hair was rough and slightly wavy, the colour dulled by rain and salt water.

Tara tried to sit up, putting a hand to the back of her head with a little groan as pain shot through it. There was a lump there the size of a bantam egg which hurt like blazes when she touched it. So don't touch it, she told herself wryly. She looked up as Mike Chandris made his way aft towards her.

'Feeling okay?' he asked, squatting beside her. 'Thought you were never going to come round.'

'I'm fine,' she assured him. 'A bit sore, that's all. You were lucky last night. We might have missed seeing you in all that rain.'

'We were all lucky last night,' he came back. 'She went down in just twenty minutes from start to finish. If that was a mine we hit, it finally got its victim after thirty-odd years.'

'How about the Captain?' Tara had already assessed that he wasn't on board. 'Did he get away?'

Mike hesitated. 'I think so. We were the last on board. He could have been picked up by one of the other boats.'

Could have, but more likely hadn't. In those conditions they'd been fortunate to pick up one man. Tara closed her eyes for a moment, remembering the big bluff captain of the *Saratoga*. It still didn't seem real. Any more than all this was real. *Shipwrecked*—a word one read in books without having any concept of its horrors.

'What about the other boats?' she asked quickly, pulling herself to a sitting position with a hand on the gunwale. 'Can you see them?'

'Not a sign. Mind you, they could be reasonably close. The sea's still running too high to be sure there's nothing out there.'

Tara could see what he meant, looking out over the limitless expanse of ocean herself. Last night's storm might have passed them by, but the waves were high enough still to conceal a dozen craft as low-lying as this one. The sun was already hot on her bare head. She put up a hand to feel the rough texture of her hair and grimaced.

'Trust a woman to worry about what she looks like!'

Mike was grinning watching her. 'Honey, with what you've got it makes damn-all difference!'

Her hand came down at once, but nothing she could do could stop the run of colour under her skin. Ridiculous to let a remark like that confuse her. It was exactly in keeping with the man who had made it. Except that one might have expected even him to be restrained by their predicament.

'How long before we're picked up, do you think?' she asked anxiously.

'Could be anytime.' There was a certain evasiveness in the reply. 'They'll be out looking for us now the weather's cleared.'

'Don't fill her up with false hopes,' Nick said brusquely, joining the two of them. 'She's old enough to be put in the picture.' His eyes found Tara's. 'The radio was still un-reliable last night. Nobody can be sure our Mayday got through. By now we must be well outside the regular ship-ping routes, so we can't count on being spotted by another ship. That leaves us two chances: air search—today if the signal got through, tomorrow or even the next day if it didn't—or striking land. The current seems to be carrying us roughly south-west according to the sun. If it continues to do that and we help out by rowing, we might make the Galapagos in a few days.'

She was silent for a long moment, gazing at him, sensing the unspoken flaws. 'Depending, surely, on where we are now?' she said with control. 'Mightn't we have been carried out too far during the storm?'

'Unlikely. The wind last night was nor'-nor'-east. If any-thing, we'll have been carried down closer to the islands.' He paused. 'We've got food and water for ten days if we're careful. More than adequate.'

Providing their calculations were right. Tara didn't need to ask what would happen if both chances failed. Beyond the Galapagos lay thousands of miles of nothing. But she was glad Nick had told her the worst. They were all in this together.

Mike was watching the other man with brooding eyes. 'Think that does any good?' he demanded.

'Yes.' Nick didn't bother to turn his head. 'Once you've faced the worst little can hurt you.' To Tara he added, 'How's the headache? Any dizziness or nausea?'

She shook her head, and wished she hadn't. 'Just a bump at the base of my skull. I must have done it when the explosion threw me. You'd have thought if I was going to pass out at all I'd have done it then.'

'Delayed reaction. It's not unknown.' He took her chin and turned her face gently to one side, parting her hair to probe with sensitive fingers around the sore area. 'Seems all right.'

'You're not a medic as well, by any chance?' The Number One's tone was sarcastic.

'No.' Further retort was obviously deemed a waste of breath. He let go of her chin and sat back on the thwart, face taut and strained in the bright morning light, the gash at his temple covered by a strip of white plaster from the boat's first aid kit. 'Think you could move up for'ard for a bit while the men rig the shelter?'

'Of course.' Tara resisted the urge to tug at her wrinkled skirt as he assisted her to her feet, grateful for his supporting arm against the movement of the boat. She could sense Mike Chandris's sneering regarding, but refused to let it bother her. This was not time for any kind of petty rivalry, even if there had been reason. Nick was doing this because to some extent he felt responsible for a fellow passenger.

'Shouldn't the Regans be with us?' she asked painfully, when he had seated her towards the middle of the boat.

'They went to the wrong station. I tried to call them, but there was too much noise. I shouldn't worry, I don't suppose they're any worse off than we are.'

'Nick ...' she was too concerned with other matters to notice that she had used his first name ... 'what chance do we really stand of being found by a search plane?'

His hesitation was brief. 'Not too good. In two or three days we could have moved beyond any possible search patterns.'

'Then you don't believe the Mayday signal got through?'

'Let's say I'm just not counting on it. I'd be very glad to be proved wrong.' He touched her shoulder. 'Back in a minute.'

She watched him step back across the thwarts to where three of the crew members struggled to get the flapping canvas erected. Mike was closer, but he didn't seem interested. The only other officer present was the young Number Three, who had an injured leg. She went to sit with him as he lay awkwardly along one of the side seats, smiling into worried brown eyes.

'Hi! Some voyage this turned out to be!'

He smiled back, the cloud lifting a fraction. 'You've got a lot of courage, Miss Smith. I wish some of it would rub off on me.'

'You're just being modest. And the name is Tara. You can't keep on calling me Miss Smith after all this.'

'All right ... Tara.' His grin was boyish, belying the growth of stubble on his chin. 'Sorry I can't sit up. Hurts like the dickens when I try.'

'Then don't.' Her glance went down to the leg neatly bandaged beneath the torn trousers. 'What did you do?'

'Smashed my knee against a block.' Anxiety was back in his voice, try as he could to conceal it. 'I'll probably be able to take off Long John Silver without props after this!'

Given the opportunity, Tara reflected, but she didn't voice the thought. 'I'm sure it won't be as bad as that,' she said on as light a note as she could manage. 'Once we're picked up you'll be fine.'

'Yes.' If he, too, knew the odds against that eventuality he kept them to himself. 'When's breakfast? I'm starving!'

Their first meal of the day was served some fifteen minutes later, consisting of a shared tin of bully beef, a handful of hard biscuits and a tin mug of water. Lunch, promised the elected 'cook' for the day, would be better providing the sea calmed enough to make lighting the portable paraffin stove a safe proposition. At least they would be able to make coffee. Meanwhile, something on the stomach was a prime target.

For Tara there was something unreal in the whole scene: any moment now she was going to wake up!

It was an estimate she was to revise over the coming few days of alternating hope and despair. If she dreamed at all it was of her life prior to the one she lived now on this tiny floating island. They had been here for ever; they would stay here for ever. Never getting anywhere because there was nowhere to go.

The nights were the worst. At least during the day there was activity of a kind: meals to see to; the rowing schedule to be maintained; the effort towards personal hygiene. But at night there was only the sea, dark and cruel and empty, taking them southwards into its limitless wastes. If there had ever really been any chance at all of hitting on the Galapagos it was past and gone now, yet no one was going to be the first to say it. They still listened for the sound of a plane, watched for a dark shape against the distant horizons, burning faces already scorched and blistered by the sun in endless quest for some sign of human life other than their own.

Fish were plentiful, and not difficult to catch with the aid of the fishing line which had been part of the emergency equipment on board. For the most part they ate them boiled, few of them relishing the raw concoctions Nick seemed to find quite palatable. It was the gutting that drew the sharks initially. After that they were never far away. Eventually everyone became accustomed to seeing a sickle fin cutting the surface about the boat, accepting it with an indifference daily growing.

Of them all only Nick refused to give in to hopelessness. Face grim behind the six-day growth of beard, he bullied and browbeat the men into rowing five hours a day, though to where no one knew. Tara accepted that he did it simply to give them something to do with their time rather than allow them to slump into total apathy. Twice she insisted on taking a turn, but the blisters which soon came up on her hands made any further effort too painful. She took over the tiller on occasion instead.

Mike Chandris seemed content enough to let someone else take control, spending most of his time in Tara's vicinity without appearing to notice her increasing aversion. Whatever faint attraction she might have felt for him once it had vanished completely along with respect for him as a man. Often she thanked her stars that they were not alone in the boat. To die was one thing; to die alongside his kind quite another. His young subordinate put him to shame. Despite the pain he must be in he never complained.

When land was finally sighted on the afternoon of the seventh day adrift they thought at first that it was a cloud on the horizon. It took Nick again to shake them all alive with an assertion that he could see mountains rising from the hazy mass.

Whether he had or not, Tara was never certain, but it got them moving towards it across the currents which had swept them this far, oars dipping with a will to survive soon vindicated by fact as the island grew steadily closer. It had to be an island because they were certainly nowhere near any land mass; it also had to be uncharted, unless they had managed to drift over two thousand miles down to Easter Isand in the southern Pacific. Whatever it was, it was land,

and after a week in an open boat the sight alone brought new life to weary hearts.

The ring of surf indicating a reef some half mile out from shore seemed unbroken at first sight. Only on coming in close and allowing the boat to drift down on the current was it possible to spot the gaps in the white water. None of them were wide, but they had little choice. It was either take the risk of having the bottom torn out of the boat or relinquish their last hope of survival at all.

They went in fast with Nick standing at the tiller to direct, eyes fastened on the crashing breakers to either side. There was an endless moment of tumult as the waves seized them, the horrible scraping of submerged rock along the starboard bow, and then they were through and racing shorewards on the crest of the very wave which had lifted them clear, seeing the narrow strip of white sand widen to form a beach fringed by palm trees and backed by hills thickly clad in forest on the lower slopes.

Oars were shipped and half a dozen willing volunteers leapt overboard into the waist deep surf to push and pull the boat up on to the shelving sand, securing the mooring rope to a thick jutting root before aiding the rest of the party ashore.

To have solid land beneath one's feet after so long in a constantly moving craft felt strange, Tara found. Her legs were wobbly, her balance almost non-existent. She sat down a few short feet away from the surf line and dug her fingers into the polished white grains, relishing the feel and the smell of security. At that moment, nothing else mattered.

'Great, isn't it?' Mike Chandris had followed her, standing over her with a smile splitting the half-formed beard, his once white uniform stained and scruffy. 'A regular home from home!'

'Better by far than another night in that boat,' she said, unable to bring herself even then to respond to him with any warmth. 'Aren't you going to go and help bring Ronny ashore?'

'They can manage.' He didn't bother to glance round. 'I reckon we've got about another hour of daylight left to get settled in for the night. First thing we'll need is a fire.'

Tara looked pointedly over his shoulder to where Nick and a couple of the other men were already gathering driftwood towards that purpose. 'Seems like somebody thought of that before you.'

'Fine.' He was unperturbed. 'They can do the donkey work and I'll run the show. That's my function.' He beckoned to another couple of the crew who responded through sheer force of habit. 'Get the knives out of the locker and go and cut down some palm fronds. We can rig up rough shelters for tonight, and make a more permanent job of it tomorrow. Bryant!' The name came out like a challenge. 'How many matches are there left?'

Nick looked up from the heap of wood he had been about to put one to. 'Three packs,' he said. 'Almost.' There was no expression on his face. He seemed to be waiting.

Mike strolled across to where the other knelt and held out a hand. 'I'll take charge of them now. We can't afford to waste them.'

Tara held her breath in the pause, then let it go again as Nick slowly handed over a couple of the precious packs. 'I'll keep this one,' he said. 'No use putting all our eggs in one basket.'

For a moment the Number One looked as if he might argue that point, then he shrugged suddenly and turned away. 'Have it your own way. Better keep that fire going all night, then we don't need to waste another match lighting it again in the morning. Green, get that fish we had left over. We'll have it baked for a change.'

Tara got up and went over to the fire as it began to blaze

up, meeting Nick's eyes with the question plain in her own. His shrug was a disclaimer.

'If he wants to assume command it's his privilege.'

She shivered for no apparent reason. 'I don't fancy having him in command of anything.'

'You'd rather take orders from me?' The smile was derisive. 'Wonderful what a week at sea can do!'

'I'd rather not take orders from *any*body,' she retorted, stung by his tone. 'We're all adult people capable of sorting out our priorities.'

'We're that all right. Some more than others. If you've any sense you'll make sure yours are to stay clear of Chandris—unless you wouldn't mind playing Eve to his Adam.'

She flushed in the fast lowering sunlight. 'Do you have to be crude?'

'I don't, but others might.' The pause held deliberation. 'You're one woman among eleven men. If we're going to be here any length of time, and that doesn't seem unlikely, the odds are going to cause friction. Show any one of us the least favouritism and the balloon will go up with a vengeance.'

Her head came up. 'Is that your way of telling me to stay away from you too?'

'No,' he said coolly, 'it's my way of telling you I'm as human as anybody else here. We all like to think of ourselves as civilised, but in some circumstances the veneer can wear very thin.'

'You sound as if you might already have experienced similar ones.' She was tense with the effort of control, fighting the urge to run to him and bury her face in his chest and beg for his protection. 'What happened then?'

'It's immaterial.' His face had closed up, his manner brusquening. 'Just remember what I've told you and don't ask for trouble.'

'And if it comes anyway?'

41

'That remains to be seen.' His glance went beyond her. 'Here comes Chandris now.'

And she was on her own. He couldn't have made that plainer. Tara mentally and physically squared her shoulders. So be it. She would show them all what she was made of!

CHAPTER FOUR

THERE was plenty of opportunity during those first days on the island to do just that. Beachcombing might be the ideal life for some, but it called for ingenuity on the part of those thrown into it piecemeal. The first reconnaissance party returned from the high ground of the interior to report a lozenge-shaped entirety some six miles by four, with no sign of any kind of human habitation. There were birds, some edible kinds of fruit, and coconuts, but no game larger than a small rat-like rodent which would hardly have constituted a mouthful had they been able to catch it.

That left them with fish still the staple diet. Good for the brain, anyway, as Nick dryly remarked. The discovery early on of a fresh water spring close by the beach removed that particular problem. They might lack for bulk, but they would neither starve nor die of thirst. For the present they had much to be thankful for.

It had rained heavily that first night on the beach, making suitable habitation a prime concern. Inside two days they had three palm-thatched dwellings erected, crude, but adequate to their needs. Tara had the smallest one to herself, set slightly back from the rest with a curtain of sorts made from woven grasses over the door.

If anyone objected to the extra work entailed in creating privacy for one member of the party there was nothing said. If anything her presence among them seemed to afford the men a stimulus against sliding into slipshod habits. Clothes had been washed and dried to a wrinkled semblance of their original appearance, and a daily bathe was the generally accepted order. There was nothing much they could do about shaving, and most already sported the makings of a fine beard. Ronny Tarrent, the young Third Officer, was the exception, the hair growing through in ginger tufts which were the bane of his life.

'The only consolation is that I can't see myself,' he moaned to Tara on the morning of their fourth day on the island. 'My chin feels like a motheaten coconut!'

Her answering smile was sympathetic. 'We none of us look so sparkling. I can't even get the tangles out of my hair any more.'

He eyed her for a moment, taking in the slender bare limbs almost the same colour as the tan dress, the vivid blue of her eyes against her skin. Like them all, she had lost weight, and the fine boning of her face was more pronounced, though not unbecomingly so; and if her hair looked somewhat unkempt it was only because fingers made a poor substitute for a comb.

'You don't have to worry,' he said with certainty. 'You still look twice as good as any other girl I ever met.'

'Thanks.' She was touched but wary. Of them all, Ronny was perhaps the most vulnerable to her presence; he had already shown that in so many little ways. Inviting him to notice her the way she had just done was hardly scheduled to lend distance to their relationship. She must be more careful. She said quickly, 'How's your leg today?'

His expression changed, acquiring the blankness she was beginning to recognise as refusal to consider the worst. 'It's fine. Hardly any pain at all now.'

'Oh, good.' Tara didn't believe it but saw no point in saying so. Nick had done all he could for the knee in keeping it free from infection, but the patella was either displaced or broken. The Third's only real hope, he had told her in a private aside, was a good surgeon if and when he reached home.

Home. The word conjured up such throat-aching pictures. It was ten days since the *Saratoga* had gone down, almost a month since she herself had left England. By now they must all be presumed dead. To all intents and purposes they were as good as. The island which at first had seemed such a haven was fast becoming a prison, yet if they left it where did they go? The memory of those days in the open boat was still too fresh to contemplate any further attempt at sailing to safety—for a while, at any rate.

She took a look along the beach from where she stood, acknowledging the wild beauty of white sand and over-hanging palms, smelling the tropical scents borne down on the breeze. This was the kind of paradise people dreamed about, but given a surfeit of it, even Eden soon began to pall. There was plenty to do if one looked for it, like Nick did, only every refinement he added to their living conditions seemed to underline the permanency of their stay. He was away in the island's interior right now with a couple of the other men trying out the primitive bows and arrows he had managed to construct. Not that it wouldn't be a welcome change if they did bring back some kind of feathered game as they hoped. They were all thoroughly sick of fish.

Mike Chandris drew her gaze as he came out from one of the huts, and her brows pulled together a fraction. There had been no single incident she could complain of since they'd landed, yet his attitude towards her grew steadily more familiar. Often she caught him watching her with that knowing look in his eyes as if they shared some kind of understanding. It annoyed her the more because there was little she could do about it. One thing she did know was that she wanted no part of Mike Chandris, friend or enemy. He was a man for whom she could feel nothing but contempt after seeing the way he had handled his self-assumed leadership. If there was a leader at all, it had to be Nick. He was the one who had organised the building, who had constructed rough tools, who had kept the men from one

45

another's throats on more than one occasion. Mike saw command as an excuse to sit back and let others get on with things. So far he had been allowed to get away with it, but Tara had a feeling that some time soon there was going to be a revolt even Nick couldn't stop.

Thinking of Nick brought a tautness in her chest. Had anyone ever really got near him? she wondered. Not even this business seemed to have touched him overmuch, or if it had he didn't show it. Unlike the rest of them he needed no one but himself. It was an enviable trait.

'I think I'll go for my swim,' she said to Ronny abruptly. 'Just make sure nobody else decides to come up the beach, will you, please?'

'Sure,' he said, and grinned. 'I'll watch them like a hawk!'

The sand was hot under her bare feet as she strolled towards the first gentle curve of the beach, the tan dress already sticking to her back with perspiration. Not for the first time she regretted the need to wear it at all when the bra and pants she was wearing beneath were a perfectly adequate substitute for a bikini. Only this was no holiday beach with dozens of other unclothed female forms around. As Nick had pointed out, to draw attention to her sex in any way could be tantamount to asking for trouble—although she doubted if ten days was long enough to have even begun chipping at the edges of that veneer of civilisation. Apart from Mike Chandris, of course. He was something else again.

Once out of sight of the camp around the curve it was a relief to strip off the dress and swish it through the water before hanging it in the sun to drip dry. The constant salt washes were making the material stiff and uncomfortable, but at least it would be clean to get into again. Somehow she would have to think of a way of collecting enough fresh water from the spring to enable her to rinse the garment through before very long.

46

The sea was like silk on her skin, warm and buoyant. She ducked down into it gratefully, raking through the tangles in her hair in a vain attempt to loosen them, but succeeding only in making matters somewhat worse. The salt again was half the trouble. She would need soap to get it properly clean, and that was something they didn't have. But at least she could rinse her hair through at the spring without too much trouble.

It was an effort to make herself leave the water, but she could hardly stay in it all morning. She reached the shelter of the palms to find her dress already almost dry, and spread palm branches to lie on while her undergarments dried on her enough to enable her to dress again. Lying there in the sun with her eyes closed she could almost believe herself on a normal holiday with a hotel just round the corner and people scattered around her. Her skin had adapted to constant exposure pretty well, considering. Providing she took reasonable care during the midday hours she seemed able to soak up as much as she wanted without burning. Without creams and lotions she would probably finish up like an old boot, but she couldn't afford to worry about that.

She was dozing when the shadow fell across her, and because the sunlight had been directly on her closed eyelids it took her a moment of narrowed concentration to recognise the identity of the man standing over her. Mike Chandris' calculating appraisal brought her sharply to a sitting position, her eyes flying to the dress hanging just out of reach before returning to meet his with forced levelness.

'Don't you have *any* consideration?' she demanded. 'You know I've been coming along here this time every day!'

'Yes, I know.' He was smiling, not pleasantly, his eyes glinting with an expression she didn't like. 'Enjoy your swim?'

'Yes.' She made a gesture towards the dress. 'Would you

47

mind getting out of here while I get something on?'

'What's the rush?' He dropped to the sand beside her, leaning an elbow to support his weight. 'You look just great as you are.' His free hand shot out as she attempted to get up, dragging her back down again and holding her there. 'I said what's the hurry? It's time you and I got acquainted— properly, I mean. We're going to be a long time together.'

'But not alone, thank goodness!' She pulled her arm free of his grasp and rolled away from him, pressing herself to her feet before he could come upright himself. 'Just leave me alone, Mike. I'm not interested. Can't you get that through your head?'

'And just who does interest you?' He had come to his feet and was facing her across the few feet of sand, face hard and dangerous. 'Bryant?'

'Don't be ridiculous!' She was hard put to keep her voice from quivering. 'He's no different from you.' It wasn't true, but if she could make him believe that was the way she felt she stood more chance of putting him off than if she began outlining the differences. 'I don't want anything to do with any of you!'

'Be realistic, honey. How long do you think it'll be before the others start getting ideas anyway?'

'They can have as many ideas as they like,' she retorted. 'I doubt if they'll try putting them into practice without encouragement.'

His laugh was short. 'You're all the encouragement any man needs! Now, come on. Be nice! Being stuck here is bad enough without denying ourselves all life's pleasures!'

'Mike.' She steeled herself not to turn and run as he approached. 'You're not really like this. Wouldn't you rather wait until a woman is ready to respond of her own free will?' The sudden change in his expression gave her incentive to go on with the ploy. 'My nerves are still a bit shattered from the explosion. Given a little more time ...' Deliberately she left the rest unsaid, forcing a smile as she assessed the conflicting emotions passing across his face. Was it going to work? It *had* to work. Long enough, at any rate, for her to get back to the others, And after that she would make sure he never had the opportunity to corner her again like this.

'You heard what she said.' The voice came from over on their right. 'She wants more time.'

Nick stood semi-concealed beneath an overhanging palm, mouth twisting as they both looked towards him. Like Mike, he wore only trousers, rolled to the knee and already torn in several places. A strip ripped from the cream silk shirt he had been wearing the night of the wreck was tied about his forehead as a sweat rag, lending him a piratical look considerably enhanced by the black hair covering his chest. All he needed now, Tara found herself thinking irrelevantly, was a patch over one eye. She hated to imagine what he must be making of the scene he'd just come upon—if he really had just appeared. For all she knew he had overheard the whole conversation. Right at the moment she couldn't decide whether that would be better or worse.

'You'd better get dressed,' he said now. 'We'll wait for you further down the beach.' His glance went to the man close by her, eyes narrowed. 'Right, Chandris?'

The other eyed him back for a long moment consideringly, then shrugged and stuck his hands in his pockets. 'Sure.'

Tara drew in a deep shuddering breath as the two of them walked off. She felt sick. Was this what it was going to be like from now on? Watching every move because one man couldn't find it in himself to leave her alone! If Nick hadn't turned up then there was no knowing what might have happened—what might still happen if her position remained static.

It was all very well Nick telling her to watch herself as he had done that first night, but how was she supposed to cope with a man so apparently devoid of principles as their self-acknowledged leader? What she needed was a protector—and the only man capable of fulfilling that role was Nick himself. Regardless of what he had said about his own inclinations, she doubted if she would ever be in any real danger from him. Not unless she herself encouraged his advances. And she was hardly likely to do that, remembering the effect one kiss of his had had on her.

They were waiting for her, as he had said, along the beach a way, not talking now, if they had been at all: two men of just about equal stature but with little else in common.

Mike's eyes went over her as she joined them, his mouth pulling into a slow smile. 'You shouldn't have bothered,' he said.

She didn't look at Nick, but she could sense his contempt, and it hurt. She had to talk to him, she thought desperately. Somehow or other she had to get him alone and explain the situation as it had really happened. Surely he would understand her reasons for making it appear that she might be prepared to respond to Mike's advances at some future date? He *must* understand!

There was no opportunity during the rest of the day because Nick made sure there couldn't be. He seemed to be steering deliberately clear of her. Mike made no such effort, but at least he made no further advances either. It was some consolation that her ploy seemed to have worked for the time being.

Ronny was profuse in his apologies for letting the First Officer follow her the way he had.

'I told him that you were having a bathe,' he said sheepishly. 'He just laughed. There was nothing I could do myself and the others didn't seem to want to interfere, so I was pretty glad when Nick put in an appearance. He set right out after him.' He paused, not looking at her. 'Hope the Number One didn't blot his copybook.'

'He didn't have time.' Nick, Tara realised, must have been on his heels, whch meant he had probably been on the scene almost from the word go. What exactly had been said she could scarcely remember, but she knew his name had been mentioned at one point. She smiled in a reassuring way. 'Don't worry about it, Ronny.'

By common consent the three pigeon-like birds Nick's party had managed to knock out of the trees were saved until the evening meal. Roasted over an open fire, they gave off an aroma which set every mouth watering, although the quantity of meat on the bones provided only a very small portion each. Fortunately, the hunting party's foray had yielded extra dividends in the shape of a root vegetable Nick called a yam which could be boiled like potatoes and was filling if nothing else. For the first time since leaving the ship, Tara retired without hunger gnawing at her insides.

Nobody stayed up late. There was nothing to stay up for once the light went and the eating was over for the day. On the other hand, most of them were up at daybreak again, unable to find any pleasure in sleeping in on beds made from palm fronds. Life had acquired a pattern in which boredom already played too great a part, despite Nick's efforts to alleviate it in various way. At least the Swiss Family Robinson had been provided with some of the refinements of civilised living.

There was a full moon when she awoke. She could see it riding low over the horizon through the open doorway of her hut. It took a moment for the significance of that clear view out to sink in; a moment in which the shadows released the shape of a man crouching close by. A hand came over her mouth as she opened it, stifling the cry before it was born.

51

'Don't start yelling,' Mike said softly, looming over her. 'It's only me.'

Was that supposed to make her feel more secure? Tara wondered, and bit the hand hard at the base of the thumb, taking her chance as it was snatched away with a curse to shout for help.

It was Nick's name she shouted, and from the speed with which he arrived he could have been waiting for the summons. Mike met him in the doorway on his way out, threw a punch at the figure blocking his exit and was next minute sprawling in the sand with a hand to his aching jaw. The rest of the men had come spilling from their respective huts, but made no attempt to interfere, standing there in the moonlight in a manner which said more plainly than words that this was a business for two and two only.

Whatever his faults, Mike Chandris was no cringer. He came up fast and low from the ground, thudding a fist into the other man's solar plexus and following through with the right ready to take him on the point of the jaw as he collapsed forward. But Nick didn't move into the punch as planned; winded as he must have been, he rode it, blocking the swinging fist and countering with his own right to the unprotected jaw with all the weight of his shoulder behind it.

This time the Number One stayed down, out for the count. Without speaking a couple of the crew came over and hoisted him between them to carry him across to a hut. Also without speaking, the rest dispersed again, mood uncertain.

Only when they were alone did Nick turn his attention to Tara standing motionless in the doorway of the hut, rubbing his knuckles with the palm of his other hand.

'You all right?' he asked.

She nodded, hardly trusting her voice. 'Your hand's bleeding,' she managed at length.

'Hardly surprising.' He didn't bother to look at it. 'Fist fights are never pretty.'

'I'm sorry.' She couldn't think of anything else to say, inadequate as it seemed. She wasn't surprised to see his eyebrows lift.

'For what? Stopping yourself from being raped?'

She flushed a little, and was glad of the silvery moonlight to conceal it from him. 'I hardly think he'd have gone that far.'

'Still willing to credit him with common decency?' He sounded derisive. 'Just what does it take to convince you? Chandris didn't come to your hut at this time of night for a chat. I'd say after due consideration he decided you'd had time enough.'

She made a small appealing gesture. 'It wasn't like that. This afternoon, I mean. I was just trying to ... put him off.'

'Not all that hard.'

'That's not fair!' she burst out hotly. 'What else was I supposed to do? You're about the same size and weight, and it took *you* two punches to put him down. If I'd tried hitting him it would simply have goaded him.'

'You could have tried shouting,' he pointed out, un-moved by the outburst. 'It worked well enough just now.'

'I didn't know there was anyone in earshot.' She paused, fighting for control over the hurt that made her want to lash ou right now at *him*. 'I never thanked you for that either. You're not an easy man to show gratitude towards.'

'Probably because I'd rather not have it.' He studied her for a moment longer, then shrugged. 'No point in talking about it anyway. If you're not hurt you may as well get back to bed. I doubt if Chandris is going to feel much like bothering anybody this side of morning.'

'Nick.' It took everything she had to force herself into making the appeal, but there was no other way. 'Nick, I can't go on like this.'

He paused in the act of turning away and looked at her again, expression unrevealing.

'Like what?'

'You know what I mean. I don't have to spell it out for you.' She held his gaze for a moment or two, then sighed. 'All right, so I'm convinced. I don't trust Mike Chandris, and I'm scared of him. I'd like your help.'

His laugh was low and amused. 'You mean you want protection? What makes you so sure you wouldn't be jumping out of the frying pan into the fire?' The mockery deepened when she didn't reply. 'I see. If it has to come to a choice I'm a better one than Chandris. I'm flattered. Pity you didn't study diplomacy before you set off on this trip.'

'If it had to come to a choice, yes, you would be the better one,' she responded with frankness, ignoring the satire as best as she was able. 'Only it doesn't, does it? All I'm asking for is your help.'

'What you're asking for is a saint,' he said bluntly. 'Supposing I told you that the price of my protection, as it were, is the same as demanded by our commanding officer?'

She drew in a steadying breath. 'I wouldn't believe you.'

Something altered in his expression, turning it taut and alien. 'Then it's time you had your faith shaken.'

Tara made no sound as he pushed her backwards into the hut. She was incapable of it. She felt his arms come round her, scorching through the thin material of her dress as he brought her up to him, felt the demanding pressure of his mouth claiming hers. There was a drumming in her ears caused by the rapid beating of her heart; she could feel it thudding against his chest. When she put up her hands to press him from her it was as much in defence against her own emotions. She hardly knew whether to be glad or sorry when he let her go.

'Still want my help?' he asked into the pulsating silence.

His voice was expressionless, his face hidden by the shadows.

'Yes.' It came out as little more than a whisper. She made an effort to pull herself together. 'Yes, I do. You might shake my beliefs, but you won't destroy them. You wouldn't demean yourself by forcing a woman into anything.'

'There's a good chance I wouldn't have to,' he said with irony. 'But have it your own way. Want me to move in tonight?'

Her breath caught. 'In?' she queried. 'Here?'

'Where else? The only way I'm going to be able to hold Chandris off is by appearing to have taken over myself. He's hardly going to believe it if we're occupying separate huts.'

She was looking for a flaw in that argument, and finding none. 'What about the others?' she got out at last.

'The others?' The lift of his eyebrow was sensed rather than seen.

'Well, won't they ... I mean, how will it look?' she floundered.

'It will look,' he said with deliberation, 'exactly as it's meant to look. After what happened just now I don't think anybody is going to be too surprised.'

She bit her lips. 'There might be ... objections.'

'If there are I'll have to deal with them, won't I? That's what it's supposed to be about.' He waited a moment, then said impatiently, 'You're looking for excuses. Do you or don't you want me on your side?'

On, but not *at*. At least not constantly. Tara had a sneaking premonition that she might be better off taking her chances on her own, but she didn't have that kind of courage.

'Yes,' she said.

'Right, then I'll go and get my bedding.' His teeth gleamed briefly in the darkness. 'Serve two purposes at one go. There's just about room in here for both of us if you push right over to the side.'

He was back again almost before she had had time to re-settle her own bed, trailing the palm fronds which provided some degree of comfort when arranged over a heaped sand base. There was some element in the silence in which Nick arranged his sleeping position that kept her from asking any questions. She lay down with her face to the woven wall and waited for the movements to stop, her pulses jerking in-voluntarily when he settled on his back with a faint sigh of released breath.

It was strange having someone else with her in the hut: strange; unnerving—yet somehow not wholly unpleasant. Nick Bryant was all male, and capable of stirring in her emotions she was ill equipped to handle, but he was her only safeguard against a man she despised far more than she feared him. She wished she only understood him a little better. He was such an enigma. He had once had a wife, he still had a daughter, yet he had never once talked about either: a man to whom women were obviously no novelty, but she doubted if he ever allowed himself any emotional involvement. Used was the word which sprang most readily to mind, only that sounded crude, and he wasn't. When he'd kissed her just now it had been with forcefulness but not brutality. It made her wonder what it would be like to have him kiss her and mean it.

'Go to sleep.' His voice came out of the darkness at her back edged with something she couldn't define. 'I'm not going to touch you.'

Tara wasn't sure whether relief or disappointment held the upper hand at that precise moment.

CHAPTER FIVE

MIKE CHANDRIS was quiet and sullen the following morning, nursing a bruise on his jaw already acquiring a multi-hued tint. He went off on his own soon after they had eaten, taking with him one of the home-made bows and a few arrows. Despite everything, Tara felt bad about it, but there was no way she could make things better between them. Mike had brought it on himself.

The other members of the party refrained from any kind of comment on the night's happenings at all, although Tara was conscious of frequent sly glances in her direction, and the occasional ribald aside suggested by the grins with which it was received. Nick himself appeared to have taken on an added status in their eyes: not only had he downed a man they none of them cared overmuch about, but he had appropriated for himself the only female in the group. So far it didn't seem to have occurred to any of them to resent the arrangement—except perhaps for Ronny Tarrent. And that, Tara felt, was more a case of disillusionment where she was concerned than any form of jealousy.

Nick had been gone when she woke, but the bedding spread so close to her own had been all the proof she needed that the night's events had been no dream. Somewhat to her surprise, she had slept well and deeply once she had got off again. Going outside to face everybody had taken courage; the worst part of it in meeting Nick's mocking gaze. Only the two of them knew the true state of their relationship, and it apparently caused him no small amusement to see her wilt under the barrage of assumption.

But better he should laugh at her than start taking the

situation seriously. In the light of day the whole idea held pitfalls only an idiot could fail to have foreseen. Who could she turn to now if Nick decided to exercise the privileges everyone already took for granted? She could scream her head off and nobody would probably care to interfere for fear of getting his own knocked off. To place reliance on a supposed basic integrity was a foolishness in itself. Nick was an unknown quantity; unpredictable and impossible to control. He attracted her yet scared her at one and the same time. And she had placed herself entirely in his hands.

Both the days and the nights, however, remained uneventful, and gradually she found herself beginning to relax, to accept Nick's presence in the hut as a part of her life. If he was aware of the slow change in her attitude towards him, he made no comment, but on more than one occasion she caught him watching her with a cynical twist to his lips. It piqued her sometimes to realise that for him she radiated no irresistible pull; a reaction she tried to blank off but couldn't. To have him lie at her side through the long hot nights with obviously no desire to even take her in his arms was a blow not only to the ego but to feelings far deeper than surface pride. So what did she want? she would ask herself fiercely. She should thank providence for what she had!

Mike Chandris showed no sign, so far, of contemplating a return bout with the man who had beaten him. The sullenness was still there, along with a glowering enmity whenever his glance happened to clash with Nick's, but he kept his distance—though for how long was anyone's guess.

Tempers all round were becoming frayed as the hope of early rescue slowly faded. One or two urged a further attempt to reach civilisation in the lifeboat, preferring the risks of action to the mental decay of extended life on the island. For the present they were shouted down, but it wouldn't be long before others joined them in seeking

58

escape from stagnation. Tara herself knew no doubts regarding her preferences. Life here might not be all it should be, but it was at least *life*. She tried not to think beyond each day as it came.

It was on the morning of the tenth day that Nick issued the casual invitation to join him on an expedition into the hills. Tara was not loth to agree, still not trusting the Number One to any great extent without the deterrent of Nick's presence close by.

By now they all had rough sandals made from woven palm fibre to protect the tender soles of the feet off the beach itself. They wore through quickly but were easily replaced. With some ingenuity and the help of one of the knives Tara had managed to turn the tan dress into a skirt and middy blouse top which were cooler if a little uneven around the edges. They took food with them, plus a couple of coconuts for liquid needs; where they were going the coconut palm did not grow.

Nick had his bow slung over one shoulder, with the arrows, now properly flighted with feathers, held in a quiver made from a sleeve of the cream silk shirt. He had been brown before, but now his skin was the colour of rich dark teak. Moving ahead of her through the trees coating the first slopes, he looked thoroughly adapted to the primitive life. No doubt he would always adapt to whatever circumstances demanded. He was a natural survivor. Tara wished she could say the same of herself.

It was the first time she had ventured more than half a mile or so from the camp, and she found the experience exhilarating in its very diversion. The trees were widely spaced, the undergrowth luxuriant, the sun's heat filtered to a level which put a new spring in her step. When they finally emerged on the high ground towards the centre of the island the views were tremendous, each curving bay of white sand lapped by water of a dozen different shades of blue and green, the horizons vast and distant against a sky opaque with heat.

Nick pointed out their own little bay, easily identified by the lifeboat pulled up on its beach. There was little activity down there, just an occasional dragging movement of one small dark figure up and down one section of the beach.

'That's young Tarrent trying to get his leg moving,' Nick commented dispassionately.

Tara glanced at him, tall and straight and vitally fit at her side, the dark, roughly trimmed beard lending him a Viking look. 'It's never going to be normal again, is it?' she asked in subdued tones.

'He's not going to be able to bend it. Not as it is now. He needs specialist attention.'

Which he was hardly likely to get whilever they were stuck here. Her chest felt tight. At Ronny's age a permanent stiff leg would seem almost worse than no leg at all.

Nick had seated himself on a convenient tussock of grass to slice the tops off the coconuts with the knife he carried. Without looking round, she said, 'Do *you* think we should try to leave?'

It was a moment before he answered. 'Some of us certainly should.'

She whipped round then, her hair tumbled over her face by the breeze, eyes widened. 'Nick, you wouldn't . . .'

'Leave you to the tender mercies of friend Chandris?' he finished for her as her voice faltered. He shrugged. 'The choice would be entirely yours.'

She swallowed. 'It isn't much of one.'

'It's all there is.' He handed her a nut with the contents already oozing out, eyes meeting hers levelly. 'We're hundreds of miles from any regular shipping lane, and stand about as much chance of being picked up from here as we do of sprouting wings. If we can rig up a sail of sorts and get lucky with the winds, we might make it to the mainland.

I'd calculate some eight hundred miles, give or take fifty.'

'That's a lot of sea. Wouldn't the Galapagos be nearer than that?'

'Nearer perhaps, but a hell of a lot harder to find. With no compass it's going to be rough guesswork anyway, but at least we've the whole South American coast to aim for.'

She sought for deterrents. 'What would you use for a sail?'

His smile was brief. 'That skirt of yours must hold three or four yards.'

'Thanks.' She couldn't find it in herself to smile back. 'And what am *I* supposed to do?'

'Get your priorities right,' he said shortly. 'If modesty means that much to you there's plenty of grass. With that amount of material plus one or two shirts we should manage to pick up some headway—especially if we supplement it with oars.'

'Providing I agree to let you have it.'

This time the smile held no banter. 'I'll take it off you myself if I have to. Can't you get it through your head that there are things more important than personal dignity? You're not being asked to go nude.'

'Not far off it!' Tara knew there was sense in the argument but resented his way of pointing it out. 'It's all very well for you to talk, but you're not ... not me,' she petered out lamely.

'Meaning I don't have your shape? You don't have to underline that fact. There isn't one of us who doesn't know every curve off by heart!' He registered the sudden sweep of heat into her face without softening. 'What would you expect? There's little else to look at. And that outfit doesn't exactly detract attention either. Didn't anyone ever tell you imagination is nine tenths of the enjoyment?'

'Stop it!' She was quivering with anger, aware of ridicule. 'You've said enough—more than enough! And you were the one who accused Mike Chandris of having no finesse!'

His eyes narrowed warningly. 'Are you drawing comparisons?'

'No.' Even in anger she could not afford to ignore the danger signals. There was no knowing which way he might jump. 'I just don't think it necessary to go to those lengths to make a point.'

'I do, if that's what it takes to get through to you.' He made a sudden impatient gesture. 'Let's leave it there, shall we? I didn't bring you up here to spend the day arguing.'

Which gave rise to the question of why exactly he *had* asked her to accompany him. And that, Tara decided, was also a subject to leave alone. She sat down nearby to drink some coconut milk, wiping her mouth on the back of her hand as she looked out over the vast expanse of blue.

'Do you think the others might have been picked up?' she asked into the silence which had fallen between them.

'Your guess is as good as mine.' His tone was emotionless. 'We can't even be sure any of the other boats got away.'

She was quiet for a long moment, remembering the Regans and Captain Anders, the dour Chief Engineer, and others. When she spoke again it was in an attempt to clear her mind of the images. 'Tell me about your island, Nick. Is it anything like this one?'

'Mataleta?' He shrugged. 'Similar. Pacific islands tend to adopt the same basic topographical detail. It's quite a bit bigger than this, and cultivated of course. We concentrate on coffee and copra.'

'You and your partner run the whole island between you?'

'With a little help from a few hundred islanders,' he said dryly. 'The white population runs to six people at present.'

'All one household?'

'Hardly. The Newalls have their own home a couple of

62

miles away on the other side of the plantation. There's just myself, my mother, and Jenny at Silverwood.'

'That's a beautiful name for a house.'

'It's a beautiful house.' The statement was without vanity. 'My grandfather built it on the site of the old one. It should last me out.'

'And your daughter?' The question was diffident.

'Naturally, if she wants it.' Very subtly his tone had changed. 'Anything else you'd like to know?'

He was not going to talk about his daughter; that much was certain. Tara made a production of cracking open her shell on a suitable stone to get at the kernel. 'You said six people,' she pointed out. 'So far you've only mentioned five —unless your partner has a child too.'

'No, there's just John and Olivia.' He sounded cool. 'We acquired a manager a few months back. Not quite the type I'd have liked, but he's shaping up well enough. It's a job finding anybody willing to stay any length of time on Mataleta. There's no entertainment apart from what we make for ourselves.'

Was that perhaps what had happened to his marriage? she wondered. Some women would find it hard to give up the outside world for a great part of their lives. But not if love played an even greater part, surely? And there was the child. What kind of woman would leave her own child voluntarily? Tara wished she dared ask if his wife were still alive, but knew it was beyond her. He gave the impression that he had already said more than he had intended.

'I hope you get home again soon,' she said, low-toned.

'If I don't it won't be for want of trying.' He studied her, leaning back on one elbow in the grass. 'How about you? Don't you want to see your home again?'

'I don't have as much to go back to.' She made her voice deliberately light. 'Not even a job. Recklessness, I think you called it.'

'Foolhardiness might be even nearer the mark. Look where it's got you up to now.'

'Ah, but look at the experience I'm getting. I might write a book about it when I get back, and become an overnight best-seller. It's got all the ingredients, hasn't it? One girl and eleven men alone on a desert island! Just think what hay the Press alone will make out of that! All it needs ...' her voice caught a little and she swallowed fiercely ... 'all it needs is for somebody to come and find us.'

'But we're not going to wait for that.' Nick held out an unexpected hand, understanding in his eyes. 'Tara, come over here.'

She stared at him as though mesmerised, mouth tremulous and vulnerable. There was comfort in that outstretched hand, security in the memory of his arms about her. Without allowing herself time for further thought she got up and went to him, dropping on to her knees at his side and putting her hand in his, head bent a little.

'We're going to get away from here,' he said slowly and softly. 'Not only that, but we're going to make it all the way. You're not going to start going to pieces now, because I won't let you. Do you understand? I won't *let* you!'

She nodded, unable to trust her voice, met his eyes with darkened blue ones and saw his expression take on some new element. When he drew her down to him she didn't resist, turning her mouth to his and letting the response come as it would. There was strength in his hands, but gentleness too. She quivered to his touch, coming alive like a candle held to the flame, shutting out all thought of the future beyond these moments. Nick mightn't love her, but she loved him. She had known it for days. If this was all she could have of him then why not let it happen? At least she would no longer be so alone.

The sudden lift of his head left her bereft. Throat tight and dry, she watched him press himself upright away from

64

her, hardly able to bring herself to form the words. 'Nick, I ...'

'Quiet!' It was a clipped command, the dark head turned skywards in a listening attitude. 'Can't you hear it?'

It took a moment for her to adjust to the new situation. 'Hear what?' Even as she said it the far-off droning sound penetrated her senses, bringing her sharply up from the ground to his side, her eyes scanning the heavens in swift desperate hope. 'That's a plane! Nick, that's a *plane*!'

'There!' His finger rammed upwards as the small silver shape swam into view. 'It's heading this way!'

'Here!' She was on her feet and ripping off the tan skirt with fingers that trembled in her haste. 'Wave this! They've got to see us. They've got to!'

'You wave it.' He was already moving towards the summit of the hill some twenty feet above them. 'We built a pyre up here for this!'

The plane was high and remote, but it was still moving towards the island. Tara waved the length of material frantically above her head with both hands, heard a crackle and a sudden *whoosh* behind and above her, and saw flames and smoke licking upwards from the top of the hill. Of course, the paraffin! They would have stored what was left of the paraffin from the boat up here to get the fire started quickly. Still waving, she took a glance down below, to see figures appearing as if by magic from the huts and surrounding trees to stare upwards into the sky. They must only just have heard it. Now they were seeing the fire; dancing and waving down the length of the beach in desperate effort. Shouts floated up on the breeze, hoarse and unintelligible.

When she looked back at the plane it was almost overhead, but showing no sign of having spotted their signals, droning on inexorably northwards. Nick joined her to watch it, standing with hands by his sides, face controlled and dispassionate.

'If they haven't seen us by now they never will,' he said.

'They've got to see us!' Tara increased her efforts with the skirt, already tasting the bitterness of defeat but unwilling to relinquish all hope. Please, oh, please, she prayed. Don't leave us here!

'He's turning!' Even Nick's control was bending now, his whole body poised taut as a bowstring as the silver shape banked suddenly to the left and came round in a sweep which would bring it right back over this side of the island. 'He's coming round for another look!'

The plane came in fast and low, sweeping overhead to the accompaniment of shouts and cheers from the assembled company below. Tara could see the pilot peering down at them, although the distance was still too great to make out any features. She wanted to scream with sheer exhilaration when he waggled his wings in acknowledgement of their presence. It was sheer anti-climax when he headed back on to his original course, climbing for height until the plane was once more a rapidly departing speck in the blue.

'He could hardly have got all of us in, even if he'd been able to put down.' Nick was watching her face as the last sound faded into the distance. 'If the weather stays good they might get a seaplane to us. Otherwise it will be a ship, which might mean another two or three days.'

She was deflated and suddenly full of doubts. 'You're sure he'll have realised we're stranded here?' she asked anxiously.

Nick's smile was a reassurance in itself. 'If he didn't he'll be reporting a new race of blonde-haired native women, which would have the same result. That was a reconnaissance plane. Ten to one he took photographs. I'd say they'd every chance of making the front pages!'

Tara glanced down at her bare tanned legs and felt herself go hot. Hastily she donned her skirt again and fastened the buttons, spending more time than necessary on pulling herself into order. When she looked up Nick was still smiling, though the mockery lacked some of its normal sting.

'Odd what a difference a word makes,' he commented. 'Only you would know that wasn't a bikini you're wearing.'

'It's me knowing that makes all the difference,' she responded wryly. 'I hope he didn't take any photographs. I'd feel awful!'

His laugh was good to hear, masculine and unrestrained. 'It takes a female to sort out priorities! Come on, we'd better get back to the beach. No point in staying on up here.'

No point, and precious little interest either. Not on his side. They'd be home and free inside a few days at the most. Why complicate matters? Tara closed her mind to the memory of those emotive moments in his arms. She should be glad, not sorry, that Providence had seen fit to intervene. She meant nothing to Nick beyond the casual passion of any man for any woman; right now he seemed to have forgotten anything had even happened between them. Well, that was all right, because it hadn't. Not in any way that mattered. It was all she had to hang on to.

The others were still capering on the beach when they reached the camp, filled with an energy they hadn't shown for days. Even the Number One seemed to have temporarily forsaken the baser side of his personality, laughing and joking with all and sundry. Ronny Tarrent looked drawn, but there was a new light of hope in his eyes. With rescue imminent there was a chance of regaining the use of his knee; that meant more to him than anything.

The high spirits were dampened a little when nightfall came without sight or sound of a plane. It took Nick's commonsense reasoning to bring things into perspective. Even if the pilot had radioed ahead it was doubtful if they could have got a rescue squad out here before dark, he pointed out, and no pilot was going to risk a landing close to an unknown section of coastline without plenty of light. He didn't mention the other possibility of having to wait several more days for a ship. There would be time enough for that when it became obvious that a plane was not going to be sent.

Tara couldn't stop torturing herself with the thought of nothing coming for them at all, although she knew it unlikely in the extreme that the pilot who had seen them would fail to report their position. This waiting was agony —intensified by the closing in of night. Nobody ate a great deal; there was too much tension in the air. Nobody expected to sleep either, but they dispersed as usual to the huts when conversation petered out.

Somehow Tara had taken it for granted that Nick would choose to return to the company of the other men now that rescue was so close. Mike Chandris was hardly likely to retrogress now. She retired earlier than anyone else, needing to be alone. When Nick came into the hut some time later as he normally did she was both dismayed and uncertain.

'You don't have to sleep in here any more,' she said in a small tight voice. 'There's no need, is there?'

'Hadn't thought about it.' His voice sounded level, but there was no telling what he might be thinking in the darkness. 'It's a bit late to start moving quarters anyway now.'

'Why?' she demanded recklessly. 'Because of what might be thought?' The pause was deliberate. 'Scared of losing face?'

The silence carried weight in a way almost tangible. When he answered it was in tones gone quiet and deadly. 'I hope you know what you're doing.'

Her breath felt trapped in her throat. 'Is that supposed to mean something to me?'

'It means,' he said, 'that if finishing what we began up there on the hill this afternoon is what you're after, you're going the right way about it. *Is* that what you want?'

'No.' She rolled over, pressing her face into the fragrant palm leaves. 'Just leave me alone, Nick!'

'So you can brood on it?' He made a small impatient sound deep in his throat. 'All right, so I took advantage of a situation. Maybe that makes me no better than Chandris in your eyes, but I wouldn't have been human if I hadn't wanted you right then. You've a beautiful body, and you're more than old enough to be made love to.'

'And I seemed willing—is that what you're trying to say?' She had come over on to her back again, staring up at the darkness with a hard lump in her throat. 'You think I came to you because I wanted you to make love to me.'

'To be fair, I don't think you knew *what* you wanted. I'd already warned you I was no plaster saint, so it shouldn't come as such a surprise that my reactions went a bit beyond the fatherly pat on the head.' His tone was dry. 'If that plane hadn't come when it did I daresay you'd know a whole lot more about life than you do right now. I wonder if the experience would have matured you any?'

'You're saying *I'm* immature?' The irony had stung. 'There's more to being adult than ... than sleeping around!'

'I agree.' The quietness of his voice was in direct contrast to her own heated one. 'There's a little thing called control, for a start. You shout at me again and I'm going to forget how old you are.' The pause was brief. 'To get back to what we were talking about, I'm no more impressed by so-called sexually liberated women than you are. If it comes to a point, most men would like to know they were first. I wasn't getting at your lack of experience in that sense. I was trying to make you see the whole thing in its proper perspective, that's all. What happened this afternoon was

69

just about inevitable under the circumstances. You needed some kind of emotional contact by way of reassurance and I supplied it. For the record, you'd probably have responded the same way to anyone else at that particular moment, I just happened to be the only one available.'

'That's very modest of you.' The retort was subdued but still managed to carry an edge.

'It's realistic. Things are different now, though. You've had your faith shaken in more ways than one. But you don't have to worry about me coming near you tonight. I'm tired.' He paused, tone hardening a little. 'Of course, you could always rile me into it. Sarcasm is one way.'

'You made your point,' she said. 'I'll keep it in mind.'

'Good.' He lay down himself with an air of finality. 'Now for God's sake get some sleep. It's going to be a long enough night as it is.'

Longer for her than for him, Tara thought achingly, listening to his steady breathing some time later. This was the very last time she would be alone like this with him, the very last chance she would ever have of being close to him. If he'd taken her in his arms a short time ago she knew she would have been lost. Not that it would have made any difference in the long run. To Nick she had been a part of an episode in his life; one he would no doubt waste little time in remembering. But to her he had become everything. How was she going to be able to cope through the days ahead?

The plane came into view at eight-thirty—a time which would be etched on the minds of them all for the rest of their days. It settled down gracefully within the reef after a preliminary reconnaissance, finishing its run several hundred yards down the beach from where they all stood waiting, and turning slowly to taxi back.

A hatch was opened and a collapsible dinghy lowered to

the calm water; two men got into it and rowed ashore, leaping out on to the sand with broad grins to meet the clamour of greeting and shake the eagerly outstretched hands.

'You folks sure have had it rough!' one said with sympathy. 'The other boats were picked up inside a couple of days. We gave up the search for this one after a fortnight. It was reckoned you'd none of you survived any longer than that. You realise the odds against fetching up on land in this area?'

'We can guess.' Nick eyed him levelly. 'Did everybody else make it?'

'Don't know for sure till we see who you've got here.' He flicked a glance over the assembled company, found Tara towards the rear and pursed his lips in a soundless whistle. 'So he got it right! Hey, honey, you're going to be big news back there, you know that? The Press already got wind of the story. There's a big crowd waiting to see you all brought in.' He scanned the rest of the group, then looked back at Nick and lifted his shoulders. 'Guess you don't have quite enough folk here to make it unanimous. The *Saratoga*'s skipper wasn't in the other boats either.'

'I see.' Apart from a faint compression about the lips, Nick showed no reaction. 'Shall we get aboard? We don't have anything to take with us, apart from what we're carrying. Nothing much we can do about the lifeboat.'

'No, sirree. Guess it'll just stay here and rot. Okay, everybody, let's get going. We can take four at a time. Three trips and we're home and dry. Who's going first?'

Tara found herself pushed goodnaturedly to the front by the men in her immediate vicinity. 'Women and children first!'

'We haven't got any kids,' somebody else shouted, and there was a playful scramble to be first in the dinghy after her to cries of 'Back, you scum!' from all quarters.

The second flier was Latin and spoke little English, but his smile spoke volumes as he handed Tara into the boat. 'You are a very brave lady,' he said.

There was little in the way of home comforts on board the plane, but nobody cared. Predictably, Nick was last on board, hoisting himself in through the hatch with an agility which betrayed his own eagerness to be away.

'First thing I'm going to want is a razor,' he remarked, fingering his beard with a grimace. 'Can't imagine why anybody should grow one of these through choice!'

'Think I might keep mine a bit,' put in someone else lightheartedly. 'Never had patience to try it before. Women go for beards.'

'Specially when they hide half a face like yours,' said his nearest neighbour, and dodged a mock punch.

They had taxied to the farthest end of the bay and turned for the take-off run. Tara watched the narrow strip of beach flashing by, felt the change in motion as they came unstuck from the water, and then they were air-borne and climbing up over the south side of the island to come round on a heading for home base.

Seen from above it looked small and somehow abandoned. She watched it until it fell too far astern to be seen any more.

CHAPTER SIX

THE hotel room was comfortably furnished Spanish style, insulated from the late afternoon heat outside by softly humming air-conditioning. Wakening from a sleep which had refreshed if not entirely revitalised her, Tara lay for a while looking round it, her mind going back over the events of the past hours.

Their arrival in Panama city had been an ordeal she would not wish to repeat, with the Press clamouring for detail and people staring. Even the white coveralls provided with some thoughtfulness by the crew of the rescue plane had proved less than adequate against the assessing looks of those who had already seen the morning newspapers.

It hadn't been until they reached the hotel where accommodation had been arranged for her and Nick that they had managed to get hold of a copy. The story had made the front page, along with a blown-up print of the two of them signalling from the hill, Tara's skirt caught on the breeze like a banner, supplying its own comment on her long bare legs.

'*SARATOGA* SURVIVORS FOUND SAFE AND SOUND' the headline had proclaimed, 'British Girl's Ordeal Ended'.

Nick hadn't said much, but cynicism had touched his mouth as he had scanned the column. 'Forget it,' he had advised her. 'They'd make hay of any situation like this.'

Tara knew he was right yet found it difficult to ignore the innuendo altogether. Seeing Mike Chandris in close conversation with one of the reporters hadn't helped her towards an easy mind either. Nick was hot news already,

73

being known in these parts. If it came out that he had apparently appropriated her for his own uses while they'd been on the island the Press would have a field day. And all of her making. It didn't bear thinking about.

The Regans had returned home to England less than a week ago after waiting in vain for news of the missing members of the *Saratoga*'s complement. A cable had been despatched at once to end their uncertainty. Of the others only Captain Anders had failed to make it, and no one seemed to know exactly what had happened. Tara tried not to dwell on the suspicion that Mike Chandris had left him to fend for himself—only on his own admission he had been the last to see the Captain. She wouldn't dare mention that fact to Nick. Dan Anders had been a friend of long standing. Given any intimation at all of what might have happened he probably wouldn't wait for confirmation.

Nick. Longing swathed her heart and her mind. Loving him like this was agony enough; parting from him would be more than she could bear. But bear it she would have to when the time came. How long it would take for arrangements to be made to return her home to England she had no idea. There were traveller's cheques to be replaced, clothes to purchase, a hundred and one different formalities to complete. One of the reporters, on behalf of his newspaper, had offered her a substantial sum for the exclusive rights to her own story of the shipwreck and subsequent events. She hadn't heard what Nick had said to the man, but whatever it was it had been enough to forestall any further approaches.

A tap on the outer door caused her to draw the sheet and light cover further up around her. After the bliss of a hot shower she had felt quite unable to don the much worn and washed undergarments again, and had slipped into bed without anything on, revelling in the feel of crisp linen next to her skin after so long. For the first time she noticed that all the things she had laid on one of the chairs had gone; taken while she slept. It left her with little choice right now.

Her tentative invitation to enter brought in a maid carrying a pile of boxes and packages which she deposited in the same empty chair before turning back with a large smile to look at Tara.

'Señor Bryant say he hope all is right for the *señorita*,' she said. 'He will come in one hour to see you.'

Tara thanked her wonderingly, and got out of bed as soon as the door had closed again to pad across the cool tiles and open up the first of the packages. Inside was a selection of lingerie made from finest silk and delicately edged with lace, each garment laid in tissue which rustled deliciously as she took it out. With unsteady hands, she opened the other boxes, laying things out on the bed as she came to them. There was an Italian cotton lace trouser suit with a matching scarf in a lovely creamy beige colour, a day dress, again in silk of a shade of blue which went with her eyes; several pairs of shoes and sandals of varying colours and design, and each with matching or toning purse. Last but by no means least, there was a smaller box containing some items of cosmetics suitable for a blue-eyed blonde.

Looking at the garments spread out around her, Tara swallowed on the hard little lump in her throat. Nick had to have ordered these, even if he hadn't chosen them himself. It showed a thoughtfulness and consideration which belied the hardened cynicism of past experience. If only she could learn to understand the man who lay behind the mask he assumed for the world at large. If only ... But there wasn't going to be time, was there? In a few short days, perhaps even hours, he would be on his way back to Mataleta and she would never see him again.

She was ready and waiting in the trouser suit and a pair of pale beige sandals with slender heels before the hour was up, her newly washed and towel-dried hair brushed to a shining smoothness about her face. She wore a pale pink lipstick and a touch of blue shadow, but had contented herself with a thorough moisturising of her skin in lieu of powder. Her face in the mirror looked strange under its tan, her hair bleached almost silver in places by the sun. She had changed in more ways than just surface appearance from the girl who had set out so blithely on this never-to-be-forgotten trip, she thought wryly. Nothing could ever be quite the same again. Some day she would learn to live with the memory of these past weeks, but she wouldn't forget.

Nick arrived as she had known he would exactly on the stated time. He eyed her appraisingly when she let him into the room, coming back to her face with an approving nod.

'You look as good as new.'

'Thanks.' She was suddenly shy of him, seeing again the man of first acquaintance in an expensive lightweight suit and crisp shirt, face clean-shaven, dark hair trimmed and styled. Gold cufflinks showed at his wrists. 'I believe I have you to thank for all this too,' with a sweep of her hand to take in what she was wearing.

'Not all of it.' He was smiling faintly. 'I had to take a guess at your size.'

'But an expert one.' She turned away from him to do some unnecessary straightening of the things on the dressing table. 'I assume from what you did order that you plan on going somewhere? Or is that assuming too much?'

'Not in the least. If we're going to be stuck here for a few days we may as well make the most of it. I thought dinner out might be a better idea than eating in the hotel.'

'A few days?' Tara swung round to look at him, the quickness of the motion betraying her surprise. 'But I thought ...'

'Thought what?' he prompted as she broke off. There was a curious expression in the grey eyes. 'That I'd leave

76

you here on your own to kick your heels till things were straightened out?' He paused, tone altering a fraction. 'That's something we're going to be discussing over dinner.'

Afterwards Tara had no impression at all of the city streets through which they passed by taxi, apart from a general one of bright lights and bustling activity. The restaurant Nick had chosen was of the older type, quiet and luxurious with tables tucked away privately in alcoves. He ordered for them both at her invitation, sitting back with an air of belonging in such surroundings to study her across the table, as the waiter departed.

'Shall we eat before we talk?' he asked.

Tara lifted her shoulders, struggling to remain outwardly controlled despite the quickened beating of her heart. 'If there's something you want to discuss with me it might as well be now, I suppose. I can't see much point in waiting till later.'

'Neither can I.' His tone was perfectly level. 'I want you to come back to Mataleta with me.'

Hope sprang in her, sweet and strong, bringing a new depth to the blue gaze. 'You mean as a kind of governess to your daughter?' she hazarded.

'You could call it that, I suppose.' He sounded amused. 'I'm suggesting you marry me.'

For how long she sat there staring at him she couldn't truly have said. When she did find her voice it sounded odd. 'I—I'm not sure I understand.'

His brows lifted in the gesture she knew so well. 'What's so difficult to understand about a proposal of marriage?'

'Your ... motives,' she managed after a moment or two. She forced herself to meet his gaze. 'You're not in love with me.'

Hope died again as swiftly as it had arisen when he failed to make the desired reply. His shrug was easy. 'It isn't absolutely necessary for two people to be in love to make a

77

success of a marriage. In a lot of ways it stands a better chance of lasting without it.'

She took a steadying breath, trying not to let the hurt show. 'Isn't that rather a cold-blooded way of looking at it?'

'It's a sensible way of looking at it. Emotion only complicates a relationship.'

'You're speaking from personal experience?'

'Yes.' The statement was flat. 'I married too young and for all the wrong reasons. I don't intend to make the same mistakes again.'

She could hardly bring herself to ask the crucial question. 'You're divorced?'

Something hardened in the lean face. 'My wife died when Jenny was a few months old.'

'I'm ... sorry.'

'No reason why you should be. It was a long time ago.' The hardness was still there. 'What I'm talking about is a partnership for our mutual benefit. Jenny needs a mother, and by your own admittance you don't have anything to go back to England for.'

'What you're talking about,' she said, 'is a marriage of convenience.'

'If you like. It doesn't matter what you call it so long as the understanding is mutual. I want a wife, you want a home. That's all there is to it.' He waited, eyes on her face with an unfathomable expression. 'Well?'

She shook her head numbly, throat dry and aching. 'There has to be something else besides logic.'

'You mean you'd rather wait around for a man you could fall madly in love with yourself?' His lips twisted. 'You might find that experience less than you'd hoped for. At least we'd be starting off without any false impressions.'

'Why me?' she demanded on a sudden surge of anger. 'If a mother for Jenny is all you want I'm sure there must be plenty who'd only be too willing to accept what you're offering!'

'Maybe.' He refused to rise to the challenge. 'Only you're what she needs—someone young enough to be a friend but with the ability to stand up to her.'

'You make her sound quite a handful.'

'She is. And not for want of a firm hand either.'

'I can believe it.' The anger had given way to some other emotion less easily defined. 'Perhaps if you'd given her more of your time instead of leaving her to the care of others she wouldn't need to force you into noticing her by playing up. Did it ever occur to you that even a spanking might be preferable to being neglected by her own father?'

His eyes had narrowed. 'What makes you so sure I've neglected her?' he asked on a dangerously level note.

'You've been away two months this time, you said, and I'm sure it won't have been the first. You don't even talk about her with any real feeling!'

'You know me so well?' The question was heavy with irony. He looked at her for a long moment, then visibly brought his temper under control. 'All right, so I've been away two months—three by the time I do get home again —but it happens to be the first time I've spent longer than a few days away from the island since her mother died. The main trouble with Jenny is that she's been over-indulged by a well-meaning but near-sighted grandmother. It happens in a lot of cases where the family is incomplete. You'd be good for us all.'

'Like a buffer between the three of you, you mean.'

'No,' he said. 'Like a foundation on which we could all build.' His regard was suddenly quizzical. 'Too tall an order for you?'

Too calculated a one, she thought in numb acceptance. What Nick was offering her was almost worse in some ways than nothing at all, yet she knew already that she was going to say yes. At least as his wife she would be with him, not stuck away on the other side of the world trying desperately to forget him. And who was to say that he wouldn't come eventually to love her? Who was to say she couldn't make him forget his former marriage with its unhappy connotations?

'No,' she said, low-toned. 'All right, Nick, I'll marry you, if that's what you want.'

'Thank you.' If there was irony in the acknowledgement it was too faint to pinpoint. 'You'd better spend tomorrow getting yourself an adequate wardrobe together while I make all the arrangements. We can be married the day after and take a flight down to the Islands. We'll be on Mataleta before the weekend.'

'Will you ... warn them?'

'I already did.' His voice was dry. 'At least, I said in this morning's cable that I expected to bring back a wife. I didn't think I'd underestimated your practicality.'

'Is that what I'm being?' Tara looked down at the glass on the table before her. 'Last night you seemed to think I was anything but.'

'Last night we were talking about different things.' A smile touched his lips. 'In that way we've nothing to worry about.' He caught the faint change in her expression and the smile widened into familiar mockery. 'You didn't anticipate a celibate relationship, I hope?'

'Of course not.' If she hadn't it was because she hadn't allowed herself to think about that aspect of it at all up to now. And she wasn't going to think too much about it now either. Men didn't have to be in love to make love; he had underlined that last night. What she had to do was make her own deeper emotions suffice for the two of them. And they were strong enough. They *had* to be strong enough. Oh, God, she thought desperately, make him love me back!

The marriage took place by civil ceremony on the Tuesday afternoon, a quick private exchange of vows which left Tara feeling very little different from before. She wore a simple dress in cream linen with a wide-brimmed hat of apricot straw. When she was congratulated by the registrar, it took her a moment to realise that Bryant was her name now as well as Nick's.

It had proved impossible to get a flight out before the following day. Nick had booked a suite at a different hotel for the night in order to dodge any possible publicity, bribing the staff to keep their secret until after they had left the country. To Tara's relief he had arranged a tour of the city and its surrounds by car to take up the rest of the daylight hours, followed by dinner and dancing at a club she knew he had chosen purposely for its very lack of intimacy. He danced well but without particular interest, holding her lightly against him. Tara had a vague idea later that they had discussed the economic situation in Britain at some considerable length, yet she couldn't recall a single word. Whatever, it got the evening over without undue strain.

It was only in the taxi going back to the hotel that reality finally began to overtake her. Tonight she was to share with Nick once more, but this time as his wife with no barriers between them. He didn't love her, but he had made it clear that he would expect compliance, at the very least, with his marital demands.

Doubt welled suddenly in her throat. The barriers hadn't broken down; they were right there still in her heart, solid as a five-barred gate. How could she have imagined for one moment that such an arrangement could work?

If Nick sensed the change in her he made no comment on it. He seemed preoccupied himself. They rode the hotel lift in a silence broken only by the tuneless whistling of the attendant. The latter appeared not to notice anything amiss, but Tara was aware of his eyes following them along the corridor before the gates closed again.

She switched on the main lights as soon as she got inside the door of the suite, her voice over-animated as she said, 'How about some coffee? I expect room service is still operative.'

'Probably, but I don't think we'll bother disturbing them.' Nick's tone was light. He moved without haste towards the connecting door through to the bedroom. 'I'll go first, then I won't be hanging around while you do all the things you women seem to find so essential before you retire for the night. You can put me out a clean shirt for morning and change these links over if you want something to do while you're waiting for the bathroom. I'll leave this one on the bed.'

Tara waited until she heard the shower start running before going through to the other room. The white shirt lay where he had cast it in a crumpled heap alongside jacket and trousers. She hung up the latter garments carefully in the wardrobe, then sat down on the bed to unfasten the gold links from the cuffs of one shirt and insert them in a pristine new one taken from his suitcase. Nick had bought far less for himself than he had insisted on getting for her. She had two brand new leather cases packed full of expensive clothes—far more than she would ever have need of on an island like Mataleta, she had protested, but her words had fallen on deaf ears. She was sure he had only accompanied her on the shopping expedition at all because he had suspected her reluctance to buy more than the bare essentials.

The replacement this morning of her lost traveller's cheques through one of the city's banks had offered an opportunity to cover her expenditure eagerly seized upon. Nick's refusal to take the money from her had sparked off a heated exchange to which he put a summary stop by declining to discuss the subject any further. Which left her in possession of something over fifteen hundred pounds with little prospect of finding anything to spend it on. Nick had suggested she invest it in her own name and offered to take care of the details for her. For the present the wad of cheques lay in her handbag—less the one she had changed for dollars.

Nick had stopped her from spending more than ten apiece on presents for Jenny and his mother, saying unfairly that she'd not buy Jenny's favour with a twenty-five-dollar doll. Anyway, he had added, she was too old for dolls.

Tara doubted if any girl of nine would reject the kind of doll she had had her eye on, but wisely had refrained from voicing the opinion. She had contented herself instead with a beautifully bound and illustrated book called *The World We Live In* which she thought might appeal to a child who had spent the greater part of her young life on a small island. For her mother-in-law, not knowing her tastes and reluctant to ask, she had plumped for a safe if unimaginative stole in soft white mohair.

The shower had stopped. Jerkily she got up and hung the shirt ready in the wardrobe for wear next morning. When the bathroom door opened she was still standing there looking with fixed attention at her own travelling suit nestling side by side with the tan one.

'Okay,' Nick said, leaving the door ajar. 'It's all yours.'

He was wearing a silk dressing gown similar in colour and style to the one he had worn on board the *Saratoga* the night he had awoken her. Paler pyjamas showed beneath. His hair was towel-dried and casually brushed, the darkness softened by the muted lighting.

Tara gathered her night things without speaking and went past him into the bathroom, closing the door between them with a gathering desperation. It was getting worse, not better. That man out there was her husband, and he was a stranger. A stranger she loved, she reminded herself; only

83

even that emotion seemed to have died a death right now. For the last two days she had been carried along on the crest of a wave, and it was breaking up under her. She couldn't go through with it, she thought numbly. She'd made a terrible mistake. But it wasn't too late even now to rectify matters. They could have the marriage annulled if it wasn't consummated.

Nick was half lying, half sitting on the bed flicking through a magazine when she finally nerved herself to go through. His gaze ran lightly over her tailored blue wrap to the tips of the matching slippers, coming back to her unadorned face with a slow smile.

'You look like a schoolgirl,' he said. 'A very lovely one, though.' He held out a hand to her, much as he had done that day on the island. 'Come over here, darling.'

Darling. Such an easy endearment, and meaning nothing. She stayed where she was, her back against the jamb in a kind of self-defence. 'Nick, I'm sorry,' she said in a small halting voice. 'I—I can't.'

He didn't move for a moment, brows drawing together in a frown. 'Can't what?' he asked at last.

'You know what I mean. Don't make me grovel,' she begged. 'I ... We made a mistake. It can't work out. You have to see that yourself.'

It was difficult to assess his reactions. He still hadn't moved. '*I* made no mistake,' he said evenly. 'And it's a bit late now to start thinking you might have. You're my wife, Tara. That's a fact, not a fancy. Now, stop being ridiculous. I only said you looked a schoolgirl; I didn't expect you to start acting like one.'

'It isn't too late,' she came back pleadingly. 'We can have the marriage annulled.'

'Like hell we can!' He was sitting upright now, face taut and angry. 'My God, you've a nerve!' He studied her flushed unhappy face and softened a little. 'I don't think you know quite what you're saying. Maybe it was wrong to rush things through the way we have, but there seemed no reason to wait around any longer than we had to. Tomorrow you'll laugh at all this nonsense about annulments, I promise you.'

'I shan't feel any different tomorrow,' she denied miserably. 'Or the next day, or the next week, or any time. It wouldn't be a marriage, Nick, it would be a mockery.'

'Then it will have to be a mockery.' His voice was flat. 'And it starts right here. If you were seventeen, even eighteen, I might consider a companionable relationship until you'd had time to adjust, but I'm damned if I'll wait for a wife of twenty-two to come to terms with life!'

'You might have to.' Her chin was high, her lips set against the betraying quiver. 'Unless you don't mind being despised!'

'I'll risk it.' He came to his feet, the movement unhurried, expression anything but tender. 'Do you come over here to me, or do I come and fetch you?'

She stood for a long frozen moment, recognising the futility of further denial yet unable to take the initiative he was offering her. She saw his mouth harden ruthlessly, felt the painful hammering of her heart as he moved towards her and made one last attempt to get through to him.

'Nick, please don't. Not this way!'

'It seems to be the only way,' he said, and swung her up off the floor, eyes glittering with an unholy light. 'You're going to grow up, my sweet, whether you like it or not. I want a wife, not another daughter.'

Her stiff unresponsiveness didn't last long—he saw to that. Nick, she acknowledged hopelessly, would always see to that. The anger in him faded as her mouth warmed to his, his arms softening their hold on her yet gathering her closer at one and the same time. He roused her without urgency; with knowledge and expertise; drawing her on to forget everything but the emotions of here and now until abandonment swept over her like the incoming tide.

Later, lying spent and pliant in his arms, she tried to forget that none of what had passed between them meant anything beyond a basic physical pleasure to him. He was an expert lover, and a considerate one. More than many women had. Couldn't she settle for that for the present and stop crying for the moon?

CHAPTER SEVEN

MATALETA came into view towards late afternoon, broadening slowly into a thick green island edged with familiar white beaches, and rising to a conical-shaped mountain towards the southern end.

'Volcanic but extinct,' Nick supplied before Tara could ask. 'It's three hundred years since it last erupted.'

'Whereabouts is Silverwood?' she wanted to know.

'There.' He pointed at a spot roughly left of central, returning his hand to the rail beside hers, his other resting on her shoulder. 'We'll be landing in about half an hour.'

And meeting his family. Tara didn't want to think about that too deeply. She would take it as it came. Life was easier that way—easier and pleasanter. That was one lesson she had learned these last few days.

Standing here now on the deck of the inter-island boat with Nick at her side, she wondered why she'd ever bothered to fight against fate in the first place. She had everything a woman could want in life; a handsome, rich, exciting husband; a beautiful home; even a ready-made daughter and mother. Nothing could touch her because she knew just where she stood. There was security in that thought alone.

'Penny for them,' Nick said close to her ear. His tone was light. 'You were looking just then like someone calculating the odds on a bet.'

'I was?' she laughed. 'I never laid a bet in my life. Are you a gambler?'

'Only when I'm sure of winning.' He put both hands to her waist, his touch possessive. 'Like this.' There was a pause before he added quietly, 'No more regrets?'

'No.' She put her head back against his chest, feeling his breath in her hair. 'You don't leave any room for them. I hope Jenny likes me.'

'She may resent you a little at first. She never knew her own mother.'

She was still in his grasp, hoping he would go on from there. But he didn't. She didn't even know his first wife's name, she realised. Nor how she had died. Odd she should have felt no deeper curiosity up to now, yet she supposed understandable too. She'd had enough problems right here in the present without delving back into the past.

The marriage hadn't been a happy one, that was for certain. At least, not towards the end. Yet it had begun with love, from what Nick had said the night he'd asked her to marry him. Perhaps he was right in thinking they stood more chance of growing together gradually. Already her own emotions were changing, plumbing deeper depths than she had known existed in her. Nick's feelings for her might still be mainly physical, but they'd grown closer in these past few short days. Even discovering a mutual appreciation of good music meant a lot for two people destined to spend many hours together.

The island's main port was named Ruru, its waterfront lined with warehouses all bearing the Bryant-Newall stamp across the seaward side of their roofs. They docked accompanied by a flotilla of small craft filled with the island people who had paddled out to meet the boat and extend the traditional Polynesian greeting, stepping down the narrow gangplank into the midst of the laughing, dusky-skinned crowds. There was music and dancing on the wharf, the girls wearing ceremonial grass skirts and flower-strewn bodices, the men in lengths of gaily patterned materials. Voices blended in song sung in their own language with its lilting emotive intonations.

Tara found half a dozen leis about her neck before she

could blink, the scents from the vividly lovely flowers filling her nostrils. Nick put an arm across her shoulders to draw her forward through the pressing throngs, laughing as he greeted first one and then another of these people who shared her island home.

'This is for you,' he shouted above the swelling music. 'They're welcoming home the bride.' His head came down closer to her ear. 'Hear that song they're singing? That's wishing us many fine sons. We mustn't disappoint them, must we?'

A woman was coming towards them through the crowds, her skin almost the same colour as those all about her. She was tall like Nick, with short curly hair turned almost completely grey, her features still holding traces of a former beauty, her smile a thing of warmth and welcome which touched Tara's heart. She put her arms about her son and held him for a moment, blinking back happy tears through the smiles. He hugged her back unselfconsciously, said something to her in soft tones, then turned back to draw Tara forward.

'Say hallo to your daughter-in-law.'

Anna Bryant held out her hands, face radiant. 'My dear, if you only knew how glad I am to see you! First hearing the news of your rescue, and then Nick's cable. I could scarcely believe it! I'd despaired of his ever ...' She broke off, catching her lip between her teeth as she glanced again at her son, then quickly carrying on. 'Let's get to the car. I suppose you'll want to drive, Nick. I gave Tamu the rest of the day off.'

The islanders were reluctant to let them go, but they made it eventually, to the opulent-looking estate parked at the back of the wharf, sliding into the seats and closing the doors on the smiling, eager followers. Tara twisted in her seat to wave as Nick put the car into motion, sinking back again with a laughing face when they reached the first curve

89

in the smoothly surfaced road heading inland.

'I always thought that was just put on for the travel films,' she said. 'What a marvellous way to arrive anywhere!'

'A marvellous excuse for stopping work too,' Nick commented, but there was no real censure in his voice. 'They'll be celebrating halfway through the night.'

'And why not?' Anna Bryant's tone was bright. 'It isn't every day the island sees a bride brought home.'

'No. Only twice in eleven years.' He didn't turn his head. 'It's all right, mother, Tara isn't sensitive about Helen. She's too sensible.'

'Oh?' There was an odd inflection in the response. She added somewhat lamely, 'Good.'

Tara looked straight ahead through the windscreen, wondering what her mother-in-law would say if she knew this was the very first time Nick had mentioned his wife by name. Too sensible to be sensitive about her, was she? She only hoped he was right about that. At the moment she wasn't sure how she felt about it at all.

Nick was speaking again, on a slightly harder note. 'I gather Jenny didn't want to come to meet us.'

'I—er—couldn't find her.' There was hesitation before Anna tagged on, 'She went out to play after lunch and probably forgot the time.'

'I'm sure she did.' The pause was emphatic. 'You've had trouble with her since I cabled, haven't you?'

'No. At least, not in the way you mean.'

'How many ways are there?'

'Oh, Nick, please.' She put a hand on his shoulder, face concerned. 'Jenny's just a child; she doesn't intend to be hurtful. It's been a bad time for her while you've been missing—a bad time for all of us. You can't expect to simply spring something like this on her and ...' Once again she let the sentence trail away uncomfortably.

90

'Your mother means that you can't expect Jenny to accept me just like that out of the blue,' Tara said levelly. 'I agree with her. In fact, you said as much yourself on the boat. Let her come round at her own pace, Nick.'

'I'd intended to,' he said. 'But that doesn't excuse her refusing to come to Ruru to meet us. I'll have something to say to that young woman when she does put in an appearance.'

Not if she could help it, Tara thought, but refrained from comment, sensing distress in Anna Bryant's silence. There would be time enough to reopen the subject when they reached the house and could be alone again.

Silverwood. Nick's home, and now hers too. As once it had been Helen's, came the small voice at the back of her mind. Eleven years ago the younger Nick had brought home another bride. Had Helen too sat like this looking out at the vivid, flower-bright scenery with hope in her heart for all that a woman held dear? Or had she already seen the island as a prison closing in on her, undermining her marriage before it had properly begun?

The road had left the port area and was rising slightly, running through orderly plantations of palms blowing green against the deepening sky. Night would be with them in less than an hour, falling with customary tropical swiftness and humming with sound. Tara remembered the nights on that other island: long and warm and filled with uncertainty for the future. For a moment she almost wished they were back there right now, sharing the little hut. Except that she wouldn't have Nick's ring on her finger if they had stayed there, would she? Those days were behind them for ever. Mataleta was the island she had to learn to call home. With all its beauty that shouldn't be hard.

'How is John?' Nick asked quietly into the silence which had fallen over the three of them, and Tara felt a totally new tension spring into being.

It seemed an age before Anna answered. 'I suppose I

should have told you at once,' she said at last, 'but I didn't want to spoil your homecoming too soon.' She paused, voice catching. 'John died three weeks ago, Nick. It was very quick and very peaceful, in his sleep. It was the following day that we heard about the *Saratoga* going down. I don't need to tell you what it was like thinking you'd both gone.'

'No, you don't.' Apart from a certain tautness about his jawline, he showed no reaction to the news. 'How did Olivia take it?'

'Rather badly. None of us expected it quite so soon, prepared as we all were for the worst. She stayed at Silverwood until the funeral, but she insisted on going back to the house afterwards. She's coming over to dinner tonight. You don't mind?'

'Why should we mind? With John gone she owns quite a fair piece of Mataleta in her own right. That makes her technically my partner.'

'Yes, it does, doesn't it.' His mother sounded vaguely unhappy about it. 'Shall you buy back her share?'

'If that's what she wants. I can't force her to sell.'

'But she has nothing to stay for now.'

'No.' The negative was abrupt, the lean features closed and expressionless. 'We'll just have to see.'

Tara found her hands were clasped tightly together in her lap without being quite sure why. Olivia. There had been something ominous in the way he had said the name. Or was she imagining things? Naturally Nick was upset by the news of his partner's death, even if he didn't show it outwardly. It had dampened her more than a little, and she hadn't known John Newall except as a name. His widow deserved sympathy in her loss, not suspicion. She had been Nick's partner's wife; she could mean nothing to him apart from that—could she?

The house was tall and white, with old red tiles and a balconied upper floor. Ornamental bushes lined the gravelled drive, giving way to lawns and flower beds beautifully kept. There was a pond with lilies and a waterfall, a wide border of hibiscus and magnolia, and finally a sweep of paving under the climber-clad pillars supporting the balcony.

The car drew up in front of double doors, and Nick got out to help both women from their seats. A couple of house servants wearing spotless white slacks and shirts came out to get the luggage, smiling the wide island smiles in acknowledgement of their employer's greeting.

They entered the house via a beautifully proportioned hall with a wrought iron staircase unfurling like a fan to the upper floor. Alcoves in the white stone walls held porcelain vases filled with flowers, the colours reflected in the high polish of the occasional tables beneath. One of the doors leading off opened slowly to frame a small girl in jeans and a grubby tee-shirt, her long brown hair tangled about a face carefully blank.

'Hallo, Daddy,' she said.

'Jenny?' He was unsmiling, viewing her with displeasure. 'Is that all you have to say for yourself?'

She considered the question for a moment, then still without expression, added, 'I'm sorry for not coming to meet you. I forgot the time.'

'You mean you deliberately stayed away until it was too late. Don't lie about it into the bargain.'

'I'm *not* lying!' The denial was impassioned. 'I *did* forget! You never believe anything I say!'

'Perhaps with good reason,' he said dryly, then shrugged and shook his head. 'All right, let's shelve it for the moment. Come and meet your stepmother.'

Not like that! Tara wanted to say, seeing the look which crossed the young face. She put all the warmth she could muster into her smile. 'Hallo, Jenny.'

' 'Lo.' The blanket had come down again, with a hint of

93

mutiny in the set of her jaw. In that moment she looked, Tara thought, very much like her father. 'May I have my tea now, Gran?'

Nick opened his mouth, face dark, caught his mother's eye and abruptly closed it again. 'We'll go straight up,' he said instead. 'You might have Liah bring us up a tray.'

'Yes, all right. I've had the west room prepared for you,' she said hurriedly. 'I hope that's all right?'

'Fine.' The smile was brief. 'If it was good enough for you and my father, it's certainly good enough for us.' He took Tara's arm without another glance in his daughter's direction. 'What time is dinner?'

'I told Olivia eight-thirty. I thought you'd probably appreciate a rest before you changed.'

'You're so right.'

Tara looked back as they moved towards the stairs. 'See you later, then, Jenny. Why don't you come up after you've had your tea, and then I can give you your present. Daddy has something for you too.'

A faint spark of interest tinged the grey-blue eyes, swiftly fading as she met her father's glance.

'No bribery,' he said. 'The presents can wait till they're deserved.'

It was wrong to start an argument in front of the child, Tara reminded herself quickly. But Nick was wrong too. That wasn't the way to treat the situation. He couldn't force Jenny to respond by punishing her. All he would succeed in doing was turn her more and more against the intruder into their midst.

The landing was open to the hall below with doors leading off to the bedrooms. Nick opened the last one on the right and stood back to let her precede him, mockery touching his mouth.

'I should carry you over the threshold by rights.'

'Strictly speaking, you should have done that downstairs.'

She kept her tone light. 'It's too late now.'

'*Is* it though?' He bent without warning and swept her off her feet, striding into the room and across to drop her unceremoniously on the magnificent fourposter bed. He was smiling but without amusement, his eyes glinting with a light she found closer to anger. 'You were saying?'

'I should have known better.' She caught at his hand as he made to turn away. 'Nick, don't blame Jenny too much. I'm sure she'll come round if we don't try to push her.' She tried to make a joke out of it. 'You know, she's very like you when she grits her teeth in that way.'

'She's even more like her mother,' he said coolly. 'And I meant what I said just then. She doesn't get a thing from either of us until she learns how to behave.'

'That's cruel!' she protested.

'Sometimes it's necessary.'

'To be kind, you mean? That's an outdated maxim, for a start.'

'So I'm an outdated parent. Just don't start trying to tell me how to handle my own family.'

'Oh,' she said softly, 'I see. Well, that puts me in my place, doesn't it?'

His expression didn't alter. 'If you want to see it that way. I won't have Jenny become an issue between us, that's all.'

Tara watched him move away across the thickly piled cream carpet to the nearest of the deep wide windows with their superb views out to sea, loosening his tie as he went. She felt lost and inadequate. Arguments with Nick always went the same way. He just clamped down and refused to consider anyone's viewpoint but his own. Often he was right, but not always. And certainly not in this. Only how did she get it through to him?

It seemed policy to leave the whole subject alone for the present. She took a look about the room she was to share with him from now on. By any standards it was worth looking at, decorated in turquoise and white, with comfortably upholstered chairs forming a sitting area close to the windows, and lamps set on low tables. Flowers spilled from a huge stone urn in a corner.

'This is really lovely,' she said impulsively. 'And so big!'

'Yes.' His own glance round was cursory. 'That other door over there leads to the dressing room. The bathroom's off it.' He had taken off his suit jacket and flung it across the nearest chair. Now he stood gazing broodingly out over the tree tops. The atmosphere still wasn't right between them. Tara stood up to go to him, then paused as a tap came on the outer door.

Their luggage was closely followed by the promised tray bearing tea and sandwiches, the latter brought in by an island girl not very much older than Tara herself. She answered in English when Nick spoke to her, her accent sing-song and attractive, going out again with a wide smile in Tara's direction.

'Are you going to do the honours?' he asked with irony as the door closed. 'Your first duty task in your new home.'

'Nick, don't,' she pleaded. 'I hate it when you talk like that!'

He studied her for a moment, then gave a sudden wry shrug. 'Not a very good start, was it? I guess I simply couldn't take Jenny's acting up after hearing about John.'

'He meant a lot to you, didn't he?' Her voice was soft.

'He was an old and close friend, yes.' He moved abruptly. 'You have the tea. Right now I want something a little stronger.'

There was a decanter and glasses on a table. He poured himself a whisky and brought it back to where she had taken a seat, perching on the wide, padded window sill to toss half of it back in one gulp.

'Remedial,' he said, catching her eye. 'But not recommended.'

The swift tropical night came down like a curtain with the vanishing of the sun, the sky turning velvet soft and deep behind him, etching his features in silhouette. Stars appeared like glimmers of green fire strung across the heavens.

Tara put down her cup and went to sit beside him, resting her cheek against his shoulder. 'I'm going to love your island, Nick,' she murmured, and wished she had the courage to add, 'As I love you'. She had hoped he would put down the glass and take her in his arms, but he didn't, although his free hand came up to smooth her hair. Something unyielding in his attitude plucked the next words from her without conscious thought. 'I'd have liked to meet your partner, but it seems I'll just have to settle for meeting his widow instead.'

The tension in the hand curving her nape was fleeting but unmistakable. 'It seems so,' he agreed. He let go of her and got to his feet. 'Time we were thinking of changing. Let's have some light to start with.'

They went down at eight-fifteen, a tall man in a white dinner jacket and a girl in filmy blue whose slender frame concealed a heart heavy with a new kind of uncertainty. A car arrived outside as they reached the hall, and one of the servants ran to throw open the outer doors. Tara felt the atmosphere press in on her as a striking brunette in flame-coloured chiffon came through them. So this was Olivia. Somehow she had known how she would look. It bore out so much.

Dark eyes flicked over her in swift assessment, turning at once to Nick and taking on an added depth. 'Anna told you, I imagine?' she said. 'It isn't the way I'd have wanted you welcomed home, Nick.'

'It isn't as I imagined either.' His tone was steady, but with an underlying note Tara found hard to define. 'How are you, Olivia?'

'As well as can be expected, I suppose, under the circumstances. It's been pretty much shock on shock.' She brought her attention back to Tara again, the smile on her lips but not touching her eyes. 'You must introduce me to your wife. She and I will have a lot in common, both being English.'

'I don't think it's necessary to be formal, do you.' Tara forced herself to move forward with outheld hand. 'I was so sorry to learn about your husband. This must be a very painful time for you.'

'Yes.' Once again the tawny gaze flickered towards Nick. 'It was sooner than any of us could have anticipated, but in its own way a blessing. John wasn't the kind of man to want to linger, as you know.'

Anna Bryant came out from a room on the right, her smile warm but with a slight strain about it too. 'I thought I heard the car,' she said. 'You've driven yourself over?'

'Of course. You know how I hate to be chauffeured.' The reply was light.

'Shall we have a drink before we eat?' suggested Nick into the small pause, and slid a hand under an elbow of each of the younger women as he moved them towards the room from which his mother had emerged.

Tara registered little of what they ate for dinner, or of the room in which they sat. Everything about Silverwood was exquisite, but right now it meant no more to her than any other place. She was being over-imaginative, she kept trying to tell herself; reading meanings which didn't exist into a few simple words and gestures. Yet she knew deep down that she had imagined nothing; that the tension out there in the hall had been real and tangible, and centred between her husband and this other woman. It was still there now, despite the apparent conviviality. And Anna Bryant recognised it too.

CHAPTER EIGHT

PREDICTABLY their time on the other island was discussed, although Nick took care to gloss over the details. Tara said as little as she could get away with, conscious of Olivia's dark questioning eyes on her face with increasing frequency.

'You must have been terrified all that time,' she remarked at one point, and then after a small pause, 'But of course, you had Nick. We heard one radio report which kept going on about this 'lone girl among eleven men' theme. Not very nice to have to face that kind of innuendo after an ordeal like you'd been through, but that's the media for you. Anyway, any speculation will have little scope now.'

'On the premise that our getting married more or less confirms it and thereby reduces the curiosity value?' Nick sounded coolly amused. 'You might have a point there.' His glance moved to Tara sitting still and silent opposite him at the round dining table. 'As we were the only two passengers it was inevitable that our names should be linked. Even the crew tended to leave us pretty much to ourselves. Tired?'

The question made her start, coming as it did without change of inflection. 'A little,' she admitted.

'Then we'll make it an early night,' Olivia said. She held up a hand in smiling denial as Tara made to protest politely. 'No, really. I could use a good night's sleep myself. Nick, the car was acting up a bit on the way over. Do you think you could just run it for me and see what you think? It's probably nothing much.'

'Surely.'

He went from the room; a moment or two later they heard the car engine start up. It sounded all right to Tara, but then she was no driver. Olivia's expression was bland, her few remarks designed to pass the time rather than contribute anything purposeful. She was smoking another cigarette when Nick came back.

'It's running rough,' he agreed. 'Could be the carburettor. You'd better spend the night here and it can be put right in the morning.'

'I'd rather get home,' she said with just the right amount of hesitation. 'I know it's probably silly of me, but I feel if I give in to the loneliness over there I'll be letting John down. I'm sure it will last me out tonight.'

'We won't risk it,' he said. 'I'll drive you home, and send the car across when it's fixed.'

Olivia smiled and shrugged, and gave a wry glance in Tara's direction. 'I should have kept quiet about the whole thing. Sorry, my dear.'

Nick's expression gave nothing away as he bent to kiss his wife's cheek. 'I'll not be long,' he said. 'Don't wait for me, though. You need some rest.'

Tara tried not to look at her mother-in-law as they all went out into the hall to see their visitor out of the door. She turned towards the stairs as it closed behind the two of them, a dispirited droop to her slim shoulders.

'I think I'll go to bed, if you don't mind.'

'No, of course not.' The other woman reached out a gentle hand and touched her cheek. 'Tara, I'm so glad Nick found you. You'll be good for him in a way few others could be.' She hesitated, her expression undergoing a slight change. 'He's my son, but even I have to admit that he's not always an easy man to live with. If you love him you have to make allowances for what's past and gone.'

Tara looked at her for a long moment. 'You mean ... Helen?' she got out with difficulty.

'Yes. I knew he was talking through his hat when he said you weren't sensitive about her. No woman could fail to be. He'll have told you what happened, of course, but I wonder ...' Her voice broke off as she saw Tara's face, her brows drawing together. 'What exactly did he tell you about Helen?'

'Only that she died when Jenny was tiny.' She was hard put to keep her voice level. 'I daresay he thought that was all I needed to know.'

Anna made a small sound of impatience in her throat. 'I daresay it wouldn't have occurred to him that you were entitled to any more than the bare details. Well, I happen to disagree with him. And if he won't tell you, I will!'

'Would that be fair?' Tara was torn between her longing to hear what Nick's mother had to say, and her loyalty to the man she had married. 'I don't really think I ...'

'I'm not sure about it being fair,' Anna interrupted her firmly. 'I certainly think it necessary to your understanding of him to hear the whole story.' Her face softened, at the indecision in the blue eyes. 'Let it be my responsibility. Come on back and have some more coffee.'

Tara went with her because she was unable to stop herself. The coffee was still hot enough to offer stimulation of a sort. She refused Anna's offer to ring through for fresh, curling her fingers about her cup as she sat waiting for the older woman to speak.

'Nick was twenty-three when he brought Helen to Mataleta,' Anna said slowly. 'She was a year younger than he was, and very lovely, but I think I knew as soon as I saw her that she wouldn't be able to settle on the island for long. She just wasn't the kind of girl who could do without parties and people constantly around her. Oh, she was in love with Nick, I'm sure. She used to say he'd swept her off her feet practically overnight. The trouble was that in marriage emotion has to grow and change, and hers simply didn't. She wanted to be married to Nick, but she wanted to show him off to everyone as her husband.' There was a long pause before she continued. 'Well, of course, Nick soon tired of trips backwards and forwards between here and the mainland. After all, it's no short journey. He gave in to her for a year or so, and then he put his foot down. They'd take a six-week vacation each year on the mainland, and make one or two trips down Tahiti way during the rest of it, but in between she was to accept life right here on Mataleta. Not that he didn't make other concessions. He even brought in a manager to give himself more time to spend with her.'

'Was that before John Newall became a partner?' Tara asked as she paused again.

'Oh, no, John was already here then. They were at school together and then university. When John's parents broke up he came out here and asked Nick to let him buy a share in the island—said it was the only real home he'd ever known. But he managed his own land and workers and just shared shipping facilities with Nick. He met Olivia just over eighteen months ago down in the islands. Apparently she'd been stranded there somehow or other. A couple of months after they were married they diagnosed this rare tropical wasting disease.' Her tone subtly altered. 'Personally, I expected Olivia to up and leave him once she realised he wasn't going to get better. Nursing a progressively ailing husband calls for devotion and self-sacrifice, and I didn't think she was capable of it. I'm glad I was wrong. John worshipped her. It would have killed him inside as well as out if she'd gone.' Anna shook her head. 'But this isn't getting us any closer yours and Nick's problems, is it? How far had I got?'

'He'd brought in a manager.' Tara wasn't all that sure she wanted to hear any more. It was all too private, too personal. She also had some faint inkling of what was to come, although she hoped she was wrong.

'Ah, yes, Paul Ravel. An eminently suitable man for the

job, we all thought. Mid-thirties; very experienced; a dedicated worker and a good solid character according to all accounts.' This time the pause held deliberation. 'Until the night he took Helen and the boat and sailed them both to their deaths in a storm. It was only after we found a lot of Helen's clothes missing that we realised they'd been running off together. I suppose Paul was going to provide her with all the things she'd been missing on Mataleta.'

Tara drew in a shaky little breath. 'How terrible for Nick! Had he no suspicion at all?'

'I doubt it,' on a dry note. 'He'd have done something about it before it got that far if he had.'

'And Jenny? They made no attempt to take Jenny with them?' Tara answered her own question, voice low and shaken. 'No, of course they didn't, or she'd have been drowned along with them. Poor little Jenny!'

'Yes, poor little Jenny. It might have been better in some ways if she had gone with them.' Anna lifted a rueful pair of shoulders at Tara's swift reaction. 'I know that sounds absolutely awful, but it's true. I love my granddaughter dearly, only ...'

'Only Nick doesn't.' Tara supplied for her as she hesitated. 'Why? Because she reminds him of Helen?'

'That's a part of it. Mostly it's because he doesn't believe she's his own child.'

'Oh no!' Tara put a hand to her mouth, her eyes dark and pain-filled. She saw in her mind's eye the small tight face which had looked back at her earlier this afternoon, the grey-blue eyes and stubborn chin. 'Oh, he's wrong. I'm sure he's wrong! She even looks like him.'

'I think so too, at times, but you try persuading Nick. Not that he ever mentions it. It was something he said a long long time ago that first made me suspect his feelings. I'd say the belief was ineradicable now.'

'But it mustn't be. There has to be a way of ...' Tara

103

stopped as realisation overtook her. She could do nothing about it herself because she wasn't even supposed to know the story. Unless Nick himself decided to confide in her she was totally helpless. And Nick wouldn't, she was certain of that. So where did they go from here?

'I'm not trying to make out he's cruel to Jenny, or anything like that,' Anna went on as if she hadn't spoken. 'He's not usually as harsh with her as he was this afternoon, even when she deserves it. She's had everything a child could want, in fact.'

'Except his love.' And I, Tara thought, know the feeling. She looked up. 'Did you know he was threatening to send her away to school?'

'Yes. He hinted as much before he left. Miss Cartwright leaving was the last straw.' Her lips twitched. 'Jenny put a spider in her bed—one of the bigger variety; harmless to humans but terrifying to anyone not in the know. The poor woman was hysterical.'

'Was Jenny sorry?' asked Tara.

'Not a bit. Not even when Nick punished her for it.'

'She has his stubbornness.'

'That's very true,' Anna agreed. 'In fact, I can remember him getting up to much the same kind of mischief when he was her age, and nothing on earth would make him express regret. I've been teaching Jenny myself for four months now since Miss Cartwright left, but naturally I can only take her so far even with the help of all the books Nick had brought over.'

'Perhaps I could help sometimes?' Tara suggested diffidently.

'Well, you're certainly closer to your own school years than I am,' Anna smiled. 'Some of the modern methods are beyond me completely. It took me quite a while to work out the way they do simple addition these days! Anyway, we can sort out all that in the morning. I daresay Nick will be eager to get back to work.' She paused. 'Does what I've told you help at all, Tara?'

'It explains a great deal,' Tara answered carefully. 'I can imagine how dreadful it must have been.' She got to her feet with surprising steadiness. 'I think I'd better go up before Nick comes back. He'll wonder why I didn't take advantage of that early night.'

'And manlike come to the conclusion we've been discussing him, perhaps?' Anna's look was shrewd. 'He should have sent Tamu to drive Olivia home instead of leaving you like this on your first night here. If you have any sense you'll tell him so too.'

If she had any sense she would ignore it, Tara thought wryly. Only what was sensible about being in love? Especially when it was unrequited.

She was lying wide awake in the wide fourposter bed when the car eventually returned. It had taken Nick an hour and a half to drive a few miles and back, she calculated with numb emotion. She heard him enter the house, and the faint, far-off sound of voices. When he came up and into their room she pretended to be already asleep.

He went through to the dressing-room very quietly so as not to disturb her, and for what seemed like a century she lay there listening to the sound of the shower. He switched on no lights on coming back into the bedroom, making his way across to the bed by the silvery glow of the moon riding high over the sea. The night was hot though not sultry. Tara felt him lift the single sheet to slide under it, felt the mattress tilt a little to his weight, and then he was lying on his back with space between them, his faint sigh that of a man for whom life held problems. In that moment she hated him as she had never hated anyone in her life before.

Nick's side of the bed was empty when she woke next morning, with just the indentation left by his head in the pillow to show he had been there at all. Tara found the rest of the family breakfasting on a covered veranda at the rear of the house when she went down. Jenny kept her eyes on her plate and ignored her greeting.

'I thought I'd leave you to sleep on for a bit,' Anna said. 'We'll have some fresh coffee now that you're here.' She glanced at her granddaughter and seemed about to add something, pausing as she caught the swift shake of Tara's head. Her expression was both rueful and apologetic.

'How long has Nick been gone?' Tara asked as she took a seat at the wrought iron table.

'Oh, more than an hour. He has a lot to catch up on. Leo has done wonders considering his lack of experience, but with two estates to run this last few weeks he's had his work cut out to keep things up to scratch.'

'Leo?'

'The estate manager, Leo McKearn. Nick brought him in when John first began failing. Young, but willing and eager to learn. He's a nice boy.'

Tara digested the information for a moment before saying casually, 'If he was relatively inexperienced wasn't it rather unwise of Nick to take leave of absence for so long? Especially with John Newall unable to cope on his own.'

'He had his reasons, I'm sure.' There was an odd note in Anna's voice.

'He didn't tell you what they were?'

'Not in so many words.' The other's glance went briefly to the silent child again. 'He had business to take care of.'

'Am I going away to school?' Jenny hadn't lifted her head, but there was a faint quiver in the set of her lower lip.

'No,' Tara said before she could think about it, and got a response in the sharp lift of both heads.

'Tara . . .' Anna began, and then broke off with a helpless little gesture of her hands.

'Do you mean it, or are you just saying it?' demanded Jenny with a perception beyond her years.

'I meant it.' Might as well be hanged for a sheep as for a lamb, came the wry thought. Nick would more than likely be furious, but that was something she was going to have to deal with later. For the present it was necessary to convince Jenny she was not just trying to curry favour. 'Perhaps when you're older—say twelve—it might be a good idea to think about, but I don't see any reason why your grandmother and I can't cope between us with your lessons.'

'You?' The scowl was back, though less some of its former intensity. 'Are you a teacher as well?'

As well as what? Tara wondered humorously. 'Not a qualified one, no,' she said. 'We'd be learning together.' Oh, lord, that sounded patronising! She made a hasty attempt to add to the statement. 'It might be fun, don't you think?'

'Lessons aren't fun,' retorted her stepdaughter with emphatic rejection of the plea. 'And I don't want you to teach me. I'd rather have Gran.'

'Supposing Gran found it a bit too much for her? It isn't easy setting out a programme for a nine-year-old.'

Grey-blue eyes held hers challengingly. 'I thought you said it was fun.'

'I said it might be.' Tara was beginning to realise the problem she was up against. Jenny was both intelligent and quick, and nobody was going to put anything across on her. She was Nick all over again. Why, oh, why couldn't he see it for himself? 'It takes two to have a good time,' she tagged on lamely. 'How about showing me some of your books this morning and we could perhaps figure out something between us.'

'I don't have to do lessons on Saturdays,' came the cool reply. Jenny got up from the table. 'I'm going down to the beach.'

Tara met her mother-in-law's glance as the child's figure

departed round the corner of the veranda and pulled a wry face. 'I made a mess of that, didn't I?'

'I think you did very well considering.' Anna paused a moment. 'Apart from that bit about not going to school, that is. Nick was only saying this morning that it seemed the best thing all round. He even has one picked out for her.'

'Well, I've promised her, so I'm afraid he'll simply have to unpick it.' Tara wished she felt as confident as she sounded. 'She's too young to be sent away—and too sensitive.'

'You recognise that too.' Anna patted her hand. 'I'm sure you'll cope with the problem, my dear.'

Tara didn't ask which one.

Anna showed her round the house after they'd finished their meal. Viewing the beautiful rooms and fine furnishings, Tara wondered if there would ever come a time when she could accept Silverwood as her own home. Nick and his mother belonged here, but she was an outsider. And so, in a way, was Jenny. It gave her a sense of affiliation with the child.

Going back up to the bedroom to fetch a handkerchief about eleven-thirty, she was drawn to the windows and the view she had only gimpsed the previous night. From here it was possible to see right down on to the white curving beach where the waves curled lazily. A quarter of a mile off shore she could see the line of breakers which betokened the almost inevitable reef. All Pacific islands followed a similar pattern, she could remember Nick telling her; yet the feeling was entirely different on each.

A tiny figure came into sight, trudging along the water's edge intent upon some unidentifiable persuit. On impulse, Tara went and got into a swimsuit and robe and made her way downstairs again to find her own way to the beach.

The path led down from the west end of the terrace

108

through a belt of palms and immortelles, emerging on a smooth stretch not far up from where Jenny still searched the shallows. Tara left both sandals and robe on the sand and crossed silent-footed to the water's edge.

'Hi,' she said casually. 'Find anything interesting?'

Whether Jenny had seen her coming or not it was difficult to know, but she revealed no surprise.

'No,' she said. 'Are you going to swim?'

'Yes. If you've got a suit on under those jeans why don't you come with me?'

The reply was uncompromising. 'I don't like swimming.'

'Oh?' Tara was nonplussed for a moment. 'But you *can* swim, can't you?'

'Of course,' on a scornful note. 'Everybody can. I'm probably better than you are.'

'I wouldn't be at all surprised. I don't get a lot of practice.' Tara added lightly, 'I hope there aren't any strong currents or I'll be sunk.'

'You'll be all right this side of the reef. Even Daddy doesn't go any further than that.' Jenny seemed to consider before making the somewhat indifferent offer. 'I'll stay and watch you, if you like.'

'Yes, do, then we can walk back together.' Tara knew better than to press her luck. She waded into the beautifully warm water up to her waist, then struck out in the side-stroke she knew she did best, smiling at her own instinctive desire to impress the child.

She had done enough swimming during those ten days on the other island to have strengthened her muscles quite a bit, and now found herself able to cover quite a distance without tiring. When she finally stopped to tread water for a rest she was surprised to see how far out she had come. Jenny was a distant little figure moving back to the water's edge from the trees. Tara waved a hand and was gratified to have the signal answered.

It took longer than anticipated to regain the beach, even allowing for frequent rests on the way. By the time she did manage to pull herself up the sand she was gasping and breathless and aware of scorn in the grey-blue regard.

'You'll never be able to keep up with Daddy,' Jenny announced judiciously. 'He can swim as fast as a shark!'

'I'm sure he can.' Tara's heart ached over the pride in the young voice. Jenny's love for her father was so apparent. How could anyone fail to be moved by it? She squeezed out her hair and then shook it free again, letting it drip down the length of her back. 'I suppose I'd better get back and get changed if I'm going to be in time for lunch. It must be getting on that way by now.'

Jenny made no reply, but she could feel her close behind as she moved over to pick up the robe she had left on the sand. How she stifled the cry which sprang to her lips she never knew. The insect was the biggest she had ever seen, shaped like an oversized black clock with feelers an inch or more long questing towards the source of disturbance. With a controlled shudder she carefully shook it off, watching it scuttle to the safety of the nearest clump of grass. More afraid of her than she of it, no doubt.

'Funny it should have found its way there,' she observed without looking in Jenny's direction. 'It seems to like the grass a whole lot better than the sand.'

'It must have lost its way.' Jenny sounded a bit at a loss herself. 'Aren't you afraid of things like that? Miss Cartwright hated them. She used to scream like anything when one came near her.'

'In which case it wasn't very kind to put one in her bed, was it?' Tara suggested mildly, and saw the child's face change.

'I suppose Daddy told you about that,' she said on a subdued note.

'No.' Tara could have kicked herself for mentioning the

110

subject at all. 'As a matter of fact, it was your grandmother, but only because I asked why your governess had left so suddenly.'

'Well, I don't care,' regaining her normal defiance. 'She was horrible and I hated her! She used to tell tales about me.'

'Untrue ones?'

The pause was lengthy. 'No,' came the reluctant reply at last. 'But I didn't always do the things she said I did on purpose.'

'I'm sure you didn't.' Tara grinned suddenly. 'Nobody can be a little horror *all* the time.'

Almost Jenny grinned back. 'Is that what *you* think I am?'

'I think it's what you're trying to be. Only I won't be as easy to get rid of as the others because I love your father too.' Tara kept her voice level and matter-of-fact. 'Did it occur to you, Jenny, that I have to share him as well?'

The small face was wary. 'You mean with me?'

'And with your grandmother. Nobody can love or be loved by just one person. There are different kinds of love, that's all.' And that, Tara decided, seeing the suddenly thoughtful expression, was enough for one day. One couldn't push something like this. 'I'm going to get changed,' she said. 'Coming? You still haven't seen your present.'

Her eyes brightened. 'Daddy said I wasn't to have them until I deserved them,' she said in some hesitation.

'Well, he must decide for himself where his own is concerned, of course.' Tara mentally crossed her fingers. If this was bribery, so what? She needed every inch of advantage she could get. 'I've got one for Gran, too. We could take it down to her before lunch.'

'Yes, all right.' Jenny turned back towards the path.

It was a small victory; it might very well be an empty

one, but it was a start. Tara felt cheered despite herself.

They met no one on their way indoors. Upstairs she took the gaily wrapped parcel from the drawer where she had stored it and handed it over into frankly eager fingers. 'I hope you like it.'

The first reaction was disappointing. 'Oh,' Jenny said. 'A book.' Her voice was flat. 'I've got a lot of books already.'

'Perhaps not like this one, though.' Tara sat down beside her on the window seat and turned the pages. 'Look, it tells you all about how the earth was made and how life began. There's a section on volcanoes and another on space, then there's bits about the sea and the deserts and the rain forests, and all the different kinds of creatures who live there.'

'Oh, that's a bit like the spider I put in Miss Cartwright's bed!' Jenny exclaimed in sudden interest, putting her finger in the page. 'The one with all the hairs. It came out of a bunch of bananas.'

Tara took a look and felt in quick sympathy with the erstwhile governess. No wonder the poor woman had had hysterics!

Jenny was turning the other pages herself now, stopping now and then to examine a picture that had caught her eye. They were sitting there like that apparently absorbed when Nick came into the room.

'Cosy,' he commented, not unpleasantly, then his expression underwent an abrupt change as he realised what it was they were looking at. Tara quailed before the look he gave her, but saw no recourse other than to bluff it out.

'Jenny's been showing me the beach,' she said. 'I went for a swim.'

'So I see.' He nodded to his daughter. 'Better cut along and tidy up before lunch.'

'Can I take my book with me?' There was uncertainty in the question.

'Yes.'

Tara watched the small figure go from the room with indignation momentarily ousting any other emotion. 'You might at least have shown a little interest,' she said. 'I was just beginning to get through to her.'

'And what do *I* have to do to get through to *you*?' His voice was quiet but no less dangerous for it. 'I said she wasn't to have the book.'

'You said, I think, that she wasn't to have it until she behaved properly. I happen to think she did this morning.' Tara ignored the memory of the beetle. 'Surely I didn't have to wait for actual permission.'

'Cut out the sarcasm,' he clipped. 'This isn't a game!'

'Don't I know it!' The retort was bitter, drawing a sudden narrowing of his eyes.

'What does that mean?'

'Nothing.' Tara made a small helpless gesture of her hands. 'What it says. I know it isn't a game, Nick. It never has been for me. I married you expecting to be treated like a responsible adult, not . . .'

'Then act like one,' he cut in. 'Don't you know it's instinctive in a child to play one adult off against another? I expect you think you've got this whole thing with Jenny completely wrapped up now!'

'Of course not. Nothing is as simple as that.' She was struggling to retain some command of the situation. 'But neither is it so very complex either. Jenny doesn't misbehave through sheer naughtiness. She does it to capture attention.'

'You said that before.'

'I know I did. So why not give her a little, without making conditions? Don't you ever pick her up and hug her like most fathers do with their children.'

His face was tight and lean. 'I'm not most fathers, and Jenny isn't most children.'

'That's a very profound statement.'

113

Nick took a step towards her, then checked. 'One of these days you'll go too far,' he said. 'I'm not going to argue with you over Jenny, now, or at any other time. She can keep the book, but in future find some other way of getting round her. Hadn't you better think about getting changed?'

'Nick.' Her voice shook a little as he made to turn away. 'Don't shut me out of your life altogether.'

'Shut you out?' He had stopped to look at her, expression unrevealing. 'How do I do that? You share my name, my home ...' his mouth took on a slant ... 'and my bed. What exactly is missing?'

'Understanding.' She saw his brow lift and hurried on. 'I know we married without ... love, but at least you seemed prepared to make some attempt towards normality. You—you haven't even kissed me since we left the boat to come here yesterday.'

'Ah,' he said, 'so that's what it's all about. The bride pines for a little attention too!' He was across to her before she could move, eyes glinting with ruthless intent as he pulled her to her feet. 'That's a matter easily rectified.'

The kiss was suffocating, parting her lips to its demand, tearing her heart out in its total lack of tenderness. The anger was still there in him when he finally put her from him. 'Satisfactory—or shall we give lunch a miss?'

Tara's face was pale, her head bent. In the momentary pause she heard his sudden muffled exclamation, felt the hardness of his hands relax to draw her back against him and hold her. She didn't question the change in him; she accepted it. Anything was better than the searing violence of a moment ago.

'That was a lousy thing to do,' he said low-toned.

'It's all right.' She spoke into his chest, mouth held rigid against the hurt still filling her. 'I probably asked for it.'

'Not that way.' He ran a hand down her cheek and under her chin, lifting her face, his own dark with some emotion she couldn't fully define. 'I'm not going to start making excuses. I've had a bad morning and you bore the brunt of it, that's all.'

'Trouble?' she ventured.

'Some.' The control was back again, his tone level. 'I've been away too long.' He put his lips gently to her forehead and let her go. 'Hurry up and get dressed. We're going to be late for lunch.'

An olive branch, Tara thought painfully as she stripped off the damp swimsuit in the bathroom. Peace between them again, but at what price? She could have taken even the violence had it been aimed directly at her. But it hadn't. By his own admission their disagreement had simply triggered off the morning's frustrations.

And last night's? She closed her mind against further pain.

They had lunch on the terrace again, undercurrents masked by the demands of social contact. Nick said little about the morning's trials and Anna didn't try to press him, talking instead of the island in general, imparting snippets of local news.

'We've a big feast day coming along soon,' she told Tara. 'A kind of annual thanksgiving to the god of the volcano. They know it's dead but tradition dies harder. Were something to happen to stop the ceremony they'd blame every subsequent incident on the failure to placate him.'

Tara smiled. 'Who do they blame now?'

'They don't; they accept.' Nick's tone was unemotional. 'Precautions taken, the rest is fate. The old gods couldn't fail.'

Jenny was quiet throughout the meal. Only when it was almost over did she drop her pebble into the pool.

'Tara says I don't have to go away to school,' she announced.

In the brief but weighty pause, Tara watched a small

bright bird with a white plume on its head flutter among the branches of the nearest magnolia. When Nick answered it was not at all what she had been waiting to hear.

'If Tara says so, then no, you don't. At least not yet.'

'Do you promise?' she insisted.

This time there was no pause at all. 'Yes.'

'That's all right, then.' Her glance came over to Tara, face serious yet no longer as shuttered. 'Daddy always keeps his promises—nice ones *and* nasty ones.'

Nick's lips twitched. 'I try. What shall we do this afternoon?'

She looked from him back to Tara, and then to her grandmother. 'All of us?'

'You can count me out,' Anna said comfortably. 'I'm going to have a nice quiet read and a nap.'

'Then it will be just the three of us.' Grey eyes found blue for a moment, the irony faint but unmistakable. 'A family outing. How about showing Tara the island?'

'All right.' Jenny didn't sound over-enthusiastic, but neither did she sound totally against it.

It was better than nothing, Tara thought emotionlessly. Anything was better than nothing.

CHAPTER NINE

It was several days before Tara could say with any certainty that Jenny was beginning to accept her. Days during which progression was slow and withdrawals frequent, but nevertheless an improvement on the determined rejection of their first meeting.

A whole weekend spent with Nick had helped matters considerably. Whether what she had said to him had anything to do with it, Tara wasn't sure, but he had made some effort towards establishing a relationship between the three of them. Given both his company and his attention, Jenny had blossomed into a different child. Nick hadn't said anything, but several times Tara had seen him watching his daughter with an odd intent expression as if trying to find some point of recognition. She longed to extend reassurance herself, only that was impossible without giving Anna away. Unless he eventually confided his fears to her himself she was helpless.

Monday morning proved less of a trial than she had anticipated too. Whatever his faults, Nick had seen to it that everything possible was to hand in the schoolroom. Some basic training in actual teaching methods might have been advantageous, Tara had to acknowledge, but with some studying on her own account and commonsense application she could see no insurmountable difficulties entailed in the curriculum already laid out by her predecessor for the coming year.

The first thing she did was to transfer the classroom to the garden on every possible occasion. There might be more distractions outside, but at least they were in the fresh air.

A palm-roofed shelter overlooking the sea made an adequate store for the bulkier items of equipment, and also provided shade from the sun when necessary. By the middle of the week a routine of sorts had begun to emerge, shared by Anna on occasion but mostly involving just the two of them.

Anna's relief at being ousted from her position was too obvious to be donned as a cover-up for resentment.

'I was getting quite desperate at times,' she confessed when Tara tentatively probed her reactions. 'I was never a particularly good scholar myself, and with Jenny inclined to gloss over the bits I didn't find easy. I'm sure you'll make a far better teacher than I ever could, although it doesn't seem right somehow that you should have it to do.'

'Oh, I'm going to enjoy it,' Tara assured her quickly. 'It gives me something to do, and if it also helps bring me closer to Jenny ...' She left the rest unsaid, sensing her mother-in-law's shrewd look. Did Anna guess how much she needed to be close to *some*one? Was she aware of the distance between her son and his wife? It was hard to tell, and loyalty to Nick would not allow her to confide her fears. For the present she must bear them alone.

Olivia had not been near the house since that first night; nor had Nick mentioned her name. Yet from his leaving the house in the morning to his return sometime in the afternoon there were whole hours when Tara had no definite idea where he was. He rarely bothered to come back for lunch, she gathered from Anna. He had usually eaten either at the manager's house or with the Newalls.

Whether he still ate at the Newalls' place was open to speculation, and for Tara that meant suspicion. If he didn't call there it made Olivia an unusually reclusive person for a woman of her kind. And if he did ... She tried not to let the seeds sow themselves too deep. She had no proof that there had ever been anything beyond friendship between her husband and this one-time wife of his partner. She

118

hoped she never would have proof. To love a man was to love all facets of him, good and bad, but there had to be a limit to what one could accept without question.

It was almost the end of her first week on Mataleta before she met Leo McKearn for the first time. Nick brought him back to the house in the late afternoon, leaving him on the terrace where she and Anna were having tea while he went indoors.

'I hope you'll forgive the intrusion, Mrs Bryant,' the manager said with a formality Tara for one found rather sweet. His glance moved from one to the other as he spoke, as if not quite certain which Mrs Bryant he should be apologising to. 'Nick wants to give me some reports he's been checking, so he suggested I come back with him this afternoon.'

'I'm glad he did,' Tara smiled at him, liking his freckled, open countenance and calf-licked fair hair. Twenty-seven, Anna had said he was, she recalled. He looked younger, not the type one somehow expected to find in a job like this, especially working for someone like Nick. Sensitive, and not terribly sure of himself, she imagined. Yet he must be good at his job to have merited even the limited approval Nick had dished out that time on the island when they had discussed the subject. 'It's about time we met,' she added.

'Perhaps you'd rather have a whisky or something, Leo?' suggested Anna, on the point of filling another cup.

He shook his head. 'Tea's more my tipple, thanks—especially this early.' He took the cup from her, drank appreciatively and held on to it as he met Tara's eyes across the low table, 'You're recently out from England, I believe, Mrs Bryant?'

'Fairly,' she agreed. 'Whereabouts in Scotland do you come from?'

His smile lent charm to the thin features. 'Would you believe I've never even been to Scotland? I was born in

Reading. My parents had lived there for more than twenty years themselves with their families. The name is all that's left.'

Tara laughed. 'I thought the accent was missing, but I put it down to your having been abroad for a long time. How do you like this part of the world?'

'I love it,' he said simply. 'I was in forestry back home for a while, but the tropics always used to draw me—romanticism to a certain extent, I suppose. When you're tramping through rain and fog you tend to dream of places like this where the sun shines all day and the nights are long and warm.' Colour faintly tinged his skin beneath the light coating of tan. 'That sounds like a quote from a travel brochure, doesn't it?'

'But fair interpretation,' she responded. 'And you don't always get *that* from a travel brochure.'

'You haven't experienced one of our seasonal storms yet,' Nick said dryly, joining them. He tossed a folder down on the table in front of Leo. 'A bit messy, but the figures come out right.'

'Never was much of a hand at any kind of book-keeping.' The younger man looked uncomfortable. 'Sorry about that, Nick.'

'Yes, well, I don't suppose it's that important providing it's readable.' Nick shook his head to his mother's offer of tea. 'Not for me, thanks. I'll have a sundowner instead.'

'It isn't sundown,' she pointed out as he turned back into the house, and he glanced back with a lift of an eyebrow.

'So it isn't.'

There was cynicism in the line of his mouth when he came back carrying the heavy-based glass. 'Cheers,' he said to no one in particular, and downed half the contents in one go.

Tara kept her eyes on her teacup as he lowered himself to a seat on the arm of her chair. If he was putting on a show

120

of married conviviality for Leo's benefit she wished he wouldn't bother.

'Why don't you stay to dinner, Leo?' she said without considering it. 'You must get very lonely on your own most of the time.'

The pause seemed to stretch. 'That's very kind of you,' Leo said at last, 'but I'm hardly dressed for it.'

'You could always go home and change. It can't be more than a few miles.' She heard her own words with an odd sense of detachment. 'No place on Mataleta is more than a few miles away.'

'Yes, why not?' Nick sounded agreeable enough on the surface. 'A good idea. I'll fetch Olivia over and we'll make it a party. Come to think of it, we could do away with dinner altogether and barbecue some steaks on the beach instead. How about that?'

Leo was looking from one to the other of them a little uncertainly. It took Anna to confirm the invitation.

'It's been a long time since we last did that,' she said. 'Jenny would love it!'

'So would I.' Tara could feel steel in the arm along the back of the chair behind her head. He was angry, there was nothing more certain, but about what exactly she wasn't sure. She had given him an adequate excuse to get Olivia here; what more could he want? She got to her feet, replacing her teacup in its saucer. 'I'll go and tell Tem Gan to cancel the veal,' she said. 'Bring a pair of trunks with you, Leo, then we can make it a real beach party.'

She didn't return to the terrace after making the necessary arrangements but went instead to look for Jenny, coming across her eventually in her own room absorbed in pasting magazine cuttings into a huge scrapbook.

'Look,' she said, unsurprised by Tara's appearance in the open doorway, 'I've half filled it already!'

121

'What are you collecting?' Tara asked in some interest, and received a pitying glance.

'Pictures, of course.'

'Oh, of course.' Smiling, she added, 'We're having a barbecue on the beach tonight. Daddy says you can stay up for it.' He hadn't exactly said that, but Anna had certainly seemed to take it for granted. 'Mr McKearn is coming, and Aunt Olivia.'

'She isn't my aunt.' The statement was matter-of-fact. 'I don't like her anyway.'

Which gave them something else in common. Unaccountably Tara felt cheered. 'Well, I'm sure you'll enjoy it,' she said. 'Didn't you want any tea?'

'No.' There was a momentary pause before Jenny tagged on belatedly, 'Thank you.'

A car started up somewhere below. That would be Leo, Tara surmised. She wondered if he too had recognised the atmosphere down there on the terrace, and if so what his thoughts were right now. She had put him in a difficult position, poor man, and he wasn't the kind to take that sort of thing in his stride. Yet she could hardly apologise without underlining the fact that she had used him to get back at Nick. She doubted if he would understand her motives anyway. If it came to that she wasn't sure she understood them herself.

She purposely kept out of Nick's way for the rest of the afternoon, but she couldn't avoid him for ever. He came into their room while she was trying to decide what to wear that evening, glancing at the garments scattered around various chairs with a sardonic expression.

'Having difficulty?' he asked.

'Not really.' She tried to sound casual about it. 'It's just that I have so many things I haven't had chance to wear yet and I thought it time I went through them again.'

'If you're going to swim tonight you'll only need a suit

and a wrap,' he said, and paused. 'Unless you're counting on making an impression.'

It hadn't been an impression Tara had had in mind, more an effort towards keeping the flag flying. Nick took the initiative from her by coming across and picking out a matching one-piece suit and robe in a blue and white print. 'Wear that. It goes with your eyes. Not that Leo will see much of them in the dark—unless he gets close enough.'

'Was that necessary?' Her voice was small and tight.

'You tell me. You're the one who couldn't wait to get him back here.'

She considered him for a moment, head to one side, wondering a little at her own coolness. 'Perhaps I felt the need for some lighthearted company. Leo seems a nice uncomplicated person.'

'He's also a susceptible one. A man of his type living alone without a woman of his own is likely to fall and fall hard for the first one who shows any real interest in him.'

'Then why don't you find him a woman of his own?' she asked brightly. 'You could always advertise. Something like "Wife wanted for lonely manager on island paradise". That should bring them flocking! Don't you have the welfare of your employees at heart, Nick?'

'More than you might imagine.' The satire seemed to have amused rather than annoyed him. 'Which is precisely why I don't intend turning you loose to tie Leo up in knots. He wouldn't know what to make of your brand of backchat.'

'And you do, of course.'

'Of course. It's a cover when you're hurt or angry—or both.' He studied her kneeling on the floor before the opened drawer. 'Which is it now?'

'You mean you're not sure?' Her tone matched his for inflection. 'Then you'll just have to go on guessing.'

'Or effect a cure.' Smile mocking, he bent and lifted her upright, holding her there in front of him with his hands light about her waist. 'If you're feeling neglected it's your own fault. You've not exactly been the warm and welcoming wife these past few days.'

'Was it part of our contract that I be available at all times?' she queried huskily, and gave a small gasp of pain as his hands tightened about her middle. 'Nick, you're hurting me!'

'With intention.' If banishing the amusement from his expression had been her aim she had certainly succeeded: his eyes were cold and glittering. 'You just don't know where to draw the line, do you!' He looked at her rigidly held mouth and his own hardened accordingly. 'All right then, if it's a contract we have it's time we paid a little more attention to your side of it. I shan't ask for my dues; I'll *take* them! And that's a promise.'

'When did you ever ask?' She was trembling but determined not to back down. 'You took from the start.'

In the sudden pause the beat of her heart seemed to fill the room. There was a pitying quality in the grey regard. 'You don't even recognise the difference, do you?' he said. 'But you will. I'm sick of tiptoeing around your sensibilities!'

She took a step away from him as his grip relaxed, hardly caring what she said. 'And I'm just sick. Of you, of this whole rotten mess! I told you it wouldn't work out.'

'So you did. It seems I should have listened.' He drove his hands into his slacks pockets with a viciousness which suggested a desire to put them around her neck. 'I married you in the hope of making something good out of it. I should have realised just how much of a child you still were underneath. Well, too bad. If you won't grow up one way you'll do it another. Either way the marriage stands.'

For better or for worse, Tara thought with bitterness. All this had arisen from one relatively innocent invitation, but it had been festering there beneath the surface for days.

Nick had married her in an effort to put his partner's wife out of his mind, only to come home to find her free. It was all so obvious; it had been obvious from that very first night. Every word Olivia had uttered had betrayed the truth.

Oh, Nick had tried, she gave him his due. There had been moments of tenderness in the days they had had together before returning to Mataleta; times when she had looked into the future with real hope in her heart for a happy outcome. But it was over now, almost before it had begun. Over, yet not finished with. The marriage stands, he had said, but how could it in such circumstances? How could he even contemplate the kind of relationship he was threatening her with while loving another woman? Because he had meant it, she was certain. She could hear Jenny's voice now: 'Daddy *always* keeps his promises'.

Tara couldn't bring herself to look at the man she had married any more. She felt dead inside. He made no move to stop her as she picked up the things he had selected and walked through into the adjoining room, closing the door between them.

The beach party turned out rather differently from what she had anticipated. Word had apparently gone round to the closer communities of islanders, for they began turning up in droves soon after sundown. Fires were started on the sand and various foodstuffs produced to add to that brought down from the house. By the time the Silverwood party arrived there was singing and dancing already in progress, even the smallest children joining in the latter activity with gusto.

'It's generally accepted that any kind of outdoor event becomes a community affair,' Anna explained for Tara's benefit as Jenny disappeared into the happy, laughing throng. 'Everybody loves a party. We've had visitors here

125

who think the best part of living on a Pacific island is its people.'

Tara was inclined to agree. There was such a spirit of contentment among the Polynesians, a capacity for enjoying even the simplest pleasures to the full. She envied them the lack of complication in their lives.

Nick sat between her and Olivia to watch the revelries, his manner towards her normal enough on the surface but with an underlying edge to it she couldn't fail to recognise. Olivia looked wonderful in a flowing caftan of a lime green colour which took on luminosity in the darkness. One hardly needed to ask who *she* was trying to impress, Tara thought with cynicism, and wondered at her own lack of pain. She didn't care any more! she told herself. She had stopped caring up there in that room an hour ago. Little more than a week since her wedding day and already her love for Nick was dead—if it had ever really been alive. Perhaps love itself was only an illusion; a kind of self-hypnotism against loneliness. It was something to think about.

'What made you want a job as isolated as this one?' she asked Leo on her other side under cover of the rhythmic chanting which typified the island songs. 'Don't you ever wish for a change from all this?' signifying the sweep of beach and sea and sky with a movement of her head. 'At your age I'd have thought you'd need far more than Mata-leta can offer.'

He shook his head, smiling a little in the flickering light from the nearest fire. 'I've never been the gregarious type, Mrs Bryant. I get tongue-tied with girls, and I'm a rotten dancer.'

'You're not tongue-tied with me,' she pointed out. 'And if you can call Nick by his first name why not use mine too?'

His glance went briefly to the man beside her talking in

low tones with Olivia. 'All right, then ... Tara. You're ... well, different.'

'How?'

'You don't make me feel insignificant.'

'I don't see how anyone could do that unless you yourself already think you are,' she returned with candour, and saw his mouth twist wryly.

'Maybe that's the trouble. Up to now I haven't made much of a mark in the world. I've two brothers with top executive positions in the firms they chose to work for, plus a younger sister who's well on the way to being a qualified barrister. I didn't even make university—finished up at agricultural college instead.'

'It's a long way from that to this.'

'In some ways I suppose it is. British agriculture didn't appeal, although I quite enjoyed my stint with the Forestry Commission. Coming out here was my way of kicking over the traces, but let's face it, I only got this job because nobody else was after it at the time. I had neither the experience or the years to suit the real requirements. I only applied for it at all because it sounded so ideally my kind of thing.'

'Where were you before you came to Mataleta?' Tara wanted to know.'

'Brazil.' His grin was attractive. 'Where the nuts come from.'

'You're no nut or you wouldn't still be here. Nick once said you were shaping up very well.'

The light brown eyes warmed. 'He did? That's good to hear. Sometimes I get the impression he regrets the day he set me on.'

Don't we all, she reflected with irony. Aloud she said lightly. 'That's just his way of keeping you on your toes. He needs you as much as you need this job. He could hardly run both estates on his own.'

'Oh, I think he could if he had to. They pretty much overlap now anyway since John Newall died. Mrs Newall prefers to relay her orders through Nick.'

Tara could imagine. She took a quick glance over her shoulder, but the other two were far too engrossed in each other to overhear anything she and Leo were saying. Anna didn't appear to have noticed anything strange in the pairing off, but then Nick's mother had a way of closing her eyes to whatever she didn't want to see. It might have been better had she herself been able to cultivate the same attitude.

The food, eaten by firelight with the cicadas loud about them, tasted delicious, but Tara could conjure no real hunger. She got up after a while and wandered down to the water's edge, exchanged a few halting pleasantries with one or two or the island women and looked out to the moonlit line of the reef. The sea this side of it was smooth and silvered, shimmering like silk in cool, invitation. Without thinking about it, she shed her wrap and waded in, strking out slowly and effortlessly in an oblique line with the shore.

From the water it was a bit like looking back on a stage, setting, the firelight leaping and dancing over the brown bodies and bright-patterned clothing. She could pick out Olivia's lime green quite easily, though Nick's fawn slacks and shirt seemed to merge into the sand at her side. Leo was talking to Anna, who was wearing the soft white stole Tara had given her about her shoulders; no one appeared to have missed her at all. It was highly probable no one would miss her if she never went back.

She took herself sharply to task at that point. Feeling sorry for herself would help nothing. Nick had to be persuaded to see the futility of denying them both their freedom to start afresh. All right, divorce was a nasty word, but it was the only real solution. Why make three people unhappy for the sake of a principle? If she could fall in love with someone else herself it would make things easier. But who? There was only Leo, and much as she liked him she couldn't see that happening. In any case, it took two to be in love. She'd just proved the one-sided kind didn't work—for either party.

It was time to be going back in. Already she had moved beyond the fringe of the lighted part of the beach. She turned, treading water, felt her thigh come up against something soft and yielding and gave a low moan as a terrible burning sensation started up under her skin. The jellyfish floated by like a wraith just below the surface, tentacles trailing. Tara looked about her wildly for others, dreading a further encounter with the kind of pain spreading from her thigh right down to her knee.

She could feel the weals already rising, tender ridges running like fire beneath her fingers, stiffening the leg into immobility and bringing fear into her throat as she struggled to stay above the surface. It became a little easier when she managed to turn on to her back and float, although the pain continued to increase. By paddling with her hands she could even manage to move slowly backwards in the direction of the beach, thankful for the relative calm of the water. She felt sick, and knew tears were trickling helplessly down her cheeks to mingle with the salt already there. If only the burning would stop for a few minutes. She'd never known anything hurt worse than this!

A splashing sounded near her, and an arm came about her waist. 'What the hell do you think you're doing out here on your own?' Nick demanded furiously, treading water for them both. Then he saw her face and his own changed expression. 'What is it?'

'My leg.' It was almost a whimper. 'I—I think a jellyfish stung me.'

Nick didn't waste time in further questions. Hands suddenly gentle, he turned her on to her back again and began towing her towards the beach. He stood up as soon as he got into his depth and carried her through the shallows and the crowd of concerned brown faces to set her down on the sand in the light from the nearest fire.

The leg was a mess, the skin tight and shiny over the long red streaks, the burning intensified by contact with the air. Anna put a towel over it, pressing Tara's hand comfortingly.

'I know how much it hurts,' she said. 'I once had the same. It honestly will start to abate soon.'

Nick slid an arm under her again. 'I'll get her up to the house and put something on it. You stay down and keep things going for a bit. Leo can drive Olivia home.'

Tara was too wrapped up in her pain to pay much heed to what was happening around her. She felt Nick lift her, and turned her face into his shoulder, grateful to get away from the curious eyes and sympathetic murmurings. His arms were strong and carried her securely up through the trees and into the house.

He went straight through to the bathroom on reaching their own quarters, putting her down gently on the padded seat, then reaching out to turn on both taps to full.

'Easier to dissolve the stuff in the bath,' he said. 'That way the whole area will be covered at once.' He smoothed back the wet hair from her face, his own concerned. 'I won't be long.'

He was back within half a minute carrying a bottle of what looked like white crystals. Turning off the taps, he poured a quantity of the latter into the water and swished them around with a hand. He was still wearing swim trunks himself, his bare legs sandy where he had knelt at her side on the beach. The pain had not diminished, but neither had it grown any worse this last few minutes. Tara was able to meet his eyes with a fair degree of control as he turned back to her.

'I'll be all right now.'

His expression registered no change. 'You'll need help to get out of that suit. Best thing we can do is cut it off.'

Tara sat in frozen silence while he secured a pair of scissors from the cabinet, finding her voice again only as he came back to her. 'Nick, let me do it myself,' she whispered. 'Please.'

'You can't manage it on your own.' He glanced at her face and his mouth tightened. 'I'm not going to argue with you, Tara. This is quite ridiculous. Can you stand up?'

She did so with his help, holding on to the towel rail with the weak tears sliding down her cheeks. He cut the suit methodically down the whole of one side so that she needn't force it over the swollen thigh, helped her out of the remains of it and into the warm water, then straightened with an abruptness that betold a damped-down anger.

'Stay in there till the pain goes out of it. I'll be right next door.'

The pain subsided to a bearable level within ten minutes or so, but it was a further fifteen before Tara could bring herself to don the other thick white towelling robe and matching mules, and go through to where Nick waited.

He was standing at the window looking out towards the firelit beach. When he turned his head to look at her she couldn't meet the grey regard.

'Feeling better?' he asked.

'Much, thanks.' Her voice sounded thick and strange in her ears. She had to force herself to add in low tones, 'I— I'm sorry I was such a baby over all that, Nick. I just couldn't . . .'

'You just couldn't bear me touching you in any way after what happened this afternoon,' he finished for her levelly as her voice trailed miserably away. 'Is that what you're trying to say?'

'Something like that, I suppose.' She sat down in the nearest chair, aware of the trembling in her limbs. 'Perhaps that's a childish reaction too, but I couldn't help it.'

'A feminine reaction.' He sounded rueful. 'I didn't exactly handle the affair with finesse. I guess I was too darned mad to think much about what I was saying.'

She hesitated before asking slowly, 'Does that mean you didn't mean what you said?'

'About taking my dues?' He studied her, an odd expression in his eyes. 'Yes, I meant it all right, but not quite as I said it. I've tended to leave you to settle down to life here on Mataleta these last few days, and I think I might have been wrong about your needing that kind of break. If we'd had longer together before coming back here it might have helped towards a better understanding. Instead the gap has grown wider while we've been home. One way or another that's got to be broken down before we can start making anything of our life together. Agreed?'

'To a certain extent.' She was looking past him at the glow reflected through the window, nursing another kind of pain. 'Except that I don't happen to think that our life together stands much of a chance whatever we do. You see ...' she swallowed on the obstruction in her throat ... 'I know about Olivia.'

CHAPTER TEN

THE pause seemed to go on for ever. She daren't look at him, but she knew he was gazing fixedly at her.

'Mind if I ask exactly *what* you know about Olivia?' he said at last on a harsh note.

'The way you feel about her.' Tara still refused to lift her head. 'I'm not blaming you, Nick. You did what you thought best. You weren't to know John was going to die so soon.'

There was no movement from him. 'You seem to have it all worked out. Supposing you put it down in black and white for both of us.'

This time she had to look up. In the glow from the single lamp he had lit his face was dark and tight with some emotion beyond anger. Haltingly, she said, 'You don't deny you feel something for her?'

'I don't deny anything—or confirm it either, till I know just what it is you're getting at.'

Tara made a small gesture of appeal. 'Nick, don't make it more difficult than it already is! Falling in love with your closest friend's wife must be bad enough in normal circumstances, but you had John's illness to contend with as well. Going away was the only thing to do.'

'And marrying you?' His voice was very quiet. 'Was that the only thing to do too?'

'Yes, as you must have seen it then. I was ... available, and without any relatives who might prove troublesome.' She paused, trying to sound logical about it. 'And I suppose I seemed young enough to be moulded the way you wanted.'

'An adequate compensation, in fact?'

She flushed a little at the sarcasm. 'Not adequate enough. I haven't stopped you wanting Olivia.'

'No,' he agreed with deliberate cruelty, 'you haven't stopped me wanting Olivia. You haven't even tried to stop me wanting her. Top marks for observation, little one, but having said all that you're no nearer to understanding the situation. Sure, you were right about my reasons for taking a trip. It was either that or betray the trust of a man I thought a lot of. If it completes your record of events, I envied him Olivia from the moment he brought her back here. She's all woman.'

'And I'm not.' It was a statement, not a question, her voice low.

'No, you're not. You won't damn well let yourself be!' He shook his head in taut impatience as she attempted to speak. 'Oh, I can make you respond all right—that's elementary. I'm talking about the barriers you've erected up there in that mind of yours.'

'You can't own every last part of a person,' on a shaky note. 'I'm an individual, Nick.'

'You're my wife,' he clipped. 'If you don't like the thought of my hankering after other women then do something about it.'

She flared at him then in white-hot anger. 'I won't fight for your attentions!'

'No, you'd far rather it were the other way round. Well, you'll excuse me if I decline. Why should I bother when I can get exactly the same results by simply taking you when I feel like it?'

'And Olivia too, I suppose!'

His laugh held no humour. 'As it happens, I haven't had Olivia . . . yet. Before it was because of John, and now because I've landed myself with a wife. Strange as it may seem to you, I have some principles left.'

'If you have I'm sure you'll find a way to overcome them.'

Tara was on her feet now, steadying herself with a hand on the back of the chair, the pain in her thigh as nothing compared with the ache in her chest. 'You don't really give a damn about anyone, do you? You were hurt once and you're going to make sure it doesn't happen again, regardless of who else might get hurt in the process!'

'Is that your considered opinion?' The grey eyes were glittering, the skin about his mouth stretched white. 'A moment ago you were convinced I was in love with Olivia.'

'A moment ago I was still crediting you with normal emotions. Now ...' her voice broke a little ... 'I don't think you're capable of love, Nick. Not the way I see it.'

'And what the hell would you know about it?' He was frightening in his anger, poised as if about to descend on her. 'You married me with your eyes wide open, so don't start blabbing about finer feelings! If you weren't ...' He broke off, registering the whiteness of her face, the scarcely controlled quiver of her lips. The anger died suddenly, to be replaced by a flat civility that was infinitely worse. 'You'd better lie down before you fall down. Get into bed and I'll fetch you a couple of aspirin.'

Tara stayed rigidly where she was as he passed her to go back into the bathroom. Only when she heard him open the medicine cabinet door did she go slowly across to strip off the robe and slide into her nightdress. Her hair was still damp, but it wouldn't have to matter. Nothing mattered.

She was lying there motionless when Nick came back with the aspirin and a glass of water. She took them from him wordlessly, returning the glass to a hand which felt about as yielding as an iron bar. Only when he made to move away did her resolve break down in a shaky appeal. 'Nick, what are we going to do?'

'Precisely nothing,' he returned. 'I'll sleep in the dressing room tonight to save disturbing you. By tomorrow the poison should have worked its way out of your system.'

135

'That wasn't what I meant.'

'I'm aware of it.' He sounded weary. 'Leave well alone, Tara. We've both said a great deal too much tonight.'

'I can't leave it alone,' she said painfully. 'I—We can't go on like this.'

'There's no alternative.'

'There *has* to be an alternative.'

He came back to the bedside then, face grim as he looked down at her. 'We've been married less than a fortnight,' he said. 'I won't talk about divorce, and I won't have you talk about it either. If we can't pick up the pieces then we settle for what we do have.'

'With or without Olivia?'

His shrug was not designed to comfort. 'That's rather up to you. Perhaps if you'd worked as hard at understanding me as you have with Jenny we wouldn't be having this conversation at all.'

It was the wrong time for it, but Tara had to say it. 'Jenny needs you more than she needs anyone. It wasn't her fault that her mother ... died.'

He made an impatient movement. 'You don't know anything about it.'

'That's hardly surprising.' She had come up on one elbow, eyes dark in the pallor of her face. 'You've never told me anything, Nick. About you, *or* Helen. How can I possibly learn to understand someone who keeps as close as you do?'

His hands were in the pockets of the white robe, but she could see tension in them even through the material. 'What is there to tell? Helen was a long time ago. She doesn't affect us now.'

'She does if it was she who made you the way you are.' The expression on his face was not encouraging, but it was too late now to back out. 'You said once that you married

136

too young and for all the wrong reasons. Can love ever be entirely wrong?'

'Blind might be a better word.' He straightened abruptly. 'I'm not going to talk about Helen to you, Tara. It's in the past and it's going to stay that way. Try and get some sleep. I'm going to take a shower.'

'Why don't you go to Olivia?' she said with bitterness. 'I'm sure *she* has no difficulty whatsoever in understanding you!'

'You're so right.' He didn't bother to look back. 'Goodnight.'

The swelling and pain had gone from Tara's leg by the morning, though the marks lingered on for another twenty-four hours or so. She went through the weekend in an emotionless limbo, caring little one way or another about anything at all. If Anna recognised the symptoms of strain between her son and his wife she said nothing. It was left to Jenny to voice an opinion on the general atmosphere.

'You and Daddy have quarrelled, haven't you?' she asked Tara frankly when they were alone on the Monday morning for lessons. 'Gran said I should mind my own business and pretend not to notice, but it hasn't got any better like she said it would.' She paused, eyes wide and guileless. 'I expect you haven't started liking one another again yet.'

Tara forced a smile and tried to answer lightly. 'Of course we like one another. People don't stop doing that just because they have a difference of opinion.'

'I do.' The statement was matter-of-fact. 'I love Daddy all the time, but I don't always like him very much. He's not at all nice when he's angry.'

How true, Tara thought wryly. But then who was? There had been hard things said on both sides the other night, if she were fair about it—although on her side retaliation had been the main aim. Remembering the last hate-laden crack made her wince. If she wanted to push Nick into Olivia's obviously only too ready arms she was going exactly the right way about it.

Yet the alternative held no greater appeal. She wasn't sure she even knew *how* to fight the other woman's pull. Physical capitulation apparently wasn't enough for a man like Nick. He had to own a woman body and mind; to have her feel for him what he was incapable of feeling again for anyone. It just wasn't in her to subjugate herself to that extent—or perhaps she simply didn't feel deeply enough. Impasse whichever way one looked at it.

'How would you like to take me for a walk this afternoon?' she said. 'I thought we might go along the beach towards Ruru as far as we could then come back through the plantation.'

'All right.' Jenny gave a sudden sigh. 'Grown-ups always change the subject when they don't want to talk about something. I wish I were grown-up!'

Tara schooled her voice against any bitterness. 'Don't be in too much of a hurry. It isn't always so marvellous.'

'Oh, but that's because you're not a proper grown-up, I suppose, like Daddy and Gran,' came the prompt response. 'They're both old. Daddy is nearly thirty-five. Gran told me you're only twenty-two.'

Tara supposed she should see that 'only' as a compliment coming from a nine-year-old, but it held a cutting edge. 'Is your father's birthday very soon?' she asked.

'This week—the twenty-seventh. Haven't you got him a present?'

Tara shook her head. 'I didn't know about it before we left Panama, or I'd have bought something then.'

'Well, you'll just have to make him one, then.' With a trace of anxiety she added, 'I hope he'll like mine.'

'I'm sure he will,' Tara said with certainty. 'Can I ask what it's to be?'

'No, it's a secret.' There was a hint of the old Jenny in the blank refusal.

Tara didn't pursue the matter. Jenny was entitled to privacy. She spent her odd moments during the rest of the morning wondering what on earth she could conjure up by way of a surprise herself for the occasion. She had to give Nick something to mark the day.

As usual Nick didn't put in an appearance for lunch. Tara hadn't really expected him. She and Jenny set out about two-thirty after the sun had lowered enough to make walking a comfortable proposition, dressed almost identically in jeans and tee-shirts and carrying sandals for the return journey.

It took them about an hour to traverse the straight sweep of beach beyond their own little bay, with plenty of stops on the way to study shells and other sea debris cast up by the tide. At one point they became involved in a game similar to volleyball being played by a group of island children brought down to the beach by their teacher for the afternoon.

School hours were strictly laid down, Tara learned from the latter, a man perhaps in his early thirties who was not of island birth but hired by the estate to run the larger of the two schools. Rules were made not by Nick himself, but through a committee elected by vote from among the island populace—a kind of mini-parliament, she gathered in some fascination, with Nick only called upon when circumstances dictated the necessity for adjudication of any kind. The teacher's enthusiasm fired the interest already aroused in her through the morning sessions with Jenny, especially when he mentioned how desperately short of adequate staff both schools were, despite efforts to secure more trained people from other sources. She might not be trained herself, but there surely must be something she could do to help out. Jenny herself would benefit from the regular schooling, even if only in certain subjects. It was worth considering anyway. They both of them needed deeper interests than could be provided at Silverwood.

It was after four when they finally struck out for home through the seaward edge of the south plantation, and work was already tailing off for the day, the men gathering together in small groups to exchange idle gossip while their quotas were checked and loaded into waiting trucks. Greetings were proffered in some curiosity and surprised speculation as Tara and Jenny passed by. These people walked almost everywhere, but only with a particular purpose in mind. To do it for the simple pleasure of it seemed to be beyond their understanding.

One man said something to Jenny in his own language, pointing in a direction at right angles to the one in which they were going. Jenny replied, then looked at Tara.

'He was asking if we wanted the manager's house. It's not far from here.'

Leo's place. Tara was seized with a sudden desire to see his friendly, open face again. Leo was relatively uncomplicated compared with Nick. At least with him she didn't feel so totally inadequate.

'Let's call on him,' she said impulsively. 'I'm gasping for a long cool drink, and it's still a long way home. He might even run us back in his car.'

'I expect he will if you ask him to.' Jenny sounded agreeable enough. 'I like Mr McKearn. He's nice.'

Unmitigated approval from Jenny made him something of a rarity, Tara imagined. Even her father didn't merit that much. Without thinking about it she quickened her footsteps in the direction indicated.

The house turned out to be a bungalow, small and square and neat. There was a garden of sorts consisting of a few rows of flowers and some rather straggly shrubs around an overgrown circle of grass, and a veranda leading up from it via a couple of cement steps. Leo came hastily to his feet from a cane chair as the two of them appeared, looking both surprised and embarrassed. He was still wearing the soiled drill slacks in which he had obviously spent the day, together with a sweat-stained shirt and a disreputable pair of gym shoes. Faced with his discomfiture, Tara wished she had given a thought to their possible disruption of his routine.

'I'm sorry,' she said. 'We've ruined your rest for you. We were just passing and thought ...' She stopped in mid-sentence as the absurdity of the conventional remark struck home, the gurgle of laughter finding a response in his cautious smile. 'And thought we'd pay our respects,' she finished with what gravity she could muster when she could speak again.

'And have a lift home,' Jenny put in with the candour of her years. 'Tara got tired of walking and wanted a drink. Can I have one too, please?'

'I'll fetch you both one,' he said. 'Or at least Kim Lee will while I get into some clean clothes.' He flushed again. 'Sorry to greet you in this state. I usually flop for half an hour before I change.'

'I don't blame you. I'd do the same myself.' Tara wished she could think of something to say which would relegate the whole matter to its proper place of unimportance, though she doubted if anything she said would make things better in Leo's view. To have them catch him in his work-day grime was not a matter to be lightly dismissed if his attitude was anything to go by. Odd how one took it for granted that only women felt that way about appearances.

She was still only half way down the glass of iced lime when he returned. Jenny had wandered off round the side of the house somewhere after finishing her own drink. Spruced and fresh in crisp white slacks and a dark blue shirt, Leo seemed also to have regained some command of the situation, his manner easier as he took a seat alongside Tara's.

'That's better,' he said. 'I'd got out of the habit of caring overmuch lately.' He slanted a glance at her, lingering a moment on the curve of her mouth. 'Nick didn't mention that you were coming out this way.'

'Nick didn't know.' She kept her voice carefully casual. 'Has he been here?'

'Not since midday. He went round to the west side this afternoon.'

So at least he had not been with Olivia today. Not, Tara acknowledged, that it made a great deal of difference.

'What do you do with your time when you're not working Leo?' she asked into the pause, and saw his shoulders lift.

'Oh, nothing much. I read a lot, and listen to records. And there's the radio.'

'Don't you find it boring?'

He smiled faintly. 'You asked me that the other night. I hope you're completely over that business, by the way. It looked nasty.'

'It's quite gone now.' Tara didn't want to talk about the other night; not, at least, in relation to that particular part of it. 'You never really answered me then either, now I come to think of it.'

'I'm not lonely,' he denied after a moment. 'I've learned a little of the language while I've been here, and some of the islanders speak a little English, so I manage to communicate all right. Some of them visit me from time to time on a social basis and extend their hospitality in return. They're a very community-minded people.' He hesitated before adding, 'I've an open invitation to come over to the house when I feel like it.'

'Which you'd think twice about taking up since I arrived,' she tagged on for him shrewdly. 'Why, Leo?'

142

His laugh held a wry note. 'There's a difference between dropping in on a man and his mother and a man and his wife.'

'I fail to see it. Anna is still there—and Jenny.'

'Do you resent them being there?' He flushed again in quick embarrassment. 'I'm sorry, I shouldn't have said that. It was just that ... well, most couples have a home to themselves, for a while at least.'

'A time for adjustment,' she murmured half under her breath, then caught herself up with a jerk as she felt his gaze on her face. 'No,' she said, 'of course I don't resent them. They belong at Silverwood far more than I do.' Without really intending to, she went on, 'I was hoping you might be able to offer me some advice. You see, it's Nick's birthday in a few days and I haven't anything to give him. I mean,' she added hastily, 'I didn't realise I wouldn't be able to get anything once we'd reached Mataleta. I thought you might suggest something I could buy right here on the island. I know it's unlikely, but I can't think of any other way.'

'Well,' he said in some doubt, 'we usually order what we need from catalogues and have it shipped in via the next boat. There's a certain amount of island craftwork, of course, but nothing I can really see as being suitable for what you want.'

'Oh well, that's that, then.' She was already regretting having mentioned the subject at all. 'It was just an idea. I didn't really expect ...' She paused as his expression underwent a sudden change. 'You've thought of something?'

'Yes,' he said with some reluctance, 'but I'm not sure you'll think it very suitable yourself.' He got up. 'Excuse me a minute.'

He was back within half that time carrying a long flat box which made a heavy sound when he put it down on the wicker table between them. 'An aunt's idea of a useful

Christmas present for a man in my position,' he said with a smile. 'I've never used it, and certainly never shall.'

'It' was a carved rosewood pen-holder trimmed in silver scrollwork at each of the four corners and bearing matching pen and pencil in silver and jet. Here in this setting it looked almost laughably out of place, but Tara could see it sitting to perfection on Nick's desk in the library. It was in some real regret that she said, 'Something like that would have been ideal, Leo, but I can't possibly take a present of yours. Thanks all the same for the offer.'

'There's no reason at all why you shouldn't have it,' he responded on an eager note. 'Honestly, it's of no earthly use to me! I've carted it about with me for over a year without even opening the box. I'd be glad to be rid of it.'

Torn between two fires, Tara gazed at the stand long and hard. 'You'd have to let me pay for it,' she said at length, still in doubt. 'It must be worth at least fifty pounds.'

'Nowhere near that, I'm sure.' Leo was looking uncomfortable again. 'I'd rather you just took it—really.'

'You know I can't do that.' She bit her lip, wishing now that she had never asked in the first place. It had never occurred to her that Leo might come up with a solution of this kind to her problem. 'It's very generous of you, but I think we'd better just forget the whole thing.'

'All right,' he said with resignation, 'you can give me twenty pounds for it, if you like, and I'll buy myself a suitable replacement.'

'It's worth more than that,' she protested. 'Leo, I . . .'

'Please take it, Tara,' he broke in. 'I'm going to feel a complete idiot if you don't. Surely the actual cost isn't so important?'

It wasn't the money part of it that was worrying her quite so much as the idea of presenting Nick with a gift chosen originally for someone else *by* someone else, but she had

144

left herself with little alternative short of kicking Leo's gesture right back in his teeth.

'No, it isn't,' she agreed, and conjured a smile into his worried face. 'Thanks, Leo. Do you think you could keep it here for me for the present? I can collect it closer to the day, then there's no danger of Nick finding it first.'

'Yes, sure.' He packed the thing up again with an air of relief, leaving the package on the table. 'Would you like another drink?'

Tara shook her head. 'I think we'd better be getting back. It must be after five. Do you know where Jenny might have got to?'

'She'll be round at the back with Iggy.'

'Iggy?'

'He's a young iguana I found a while back abandoned, or lost. They become quite tame if you get them young enough. This one won't leave the place now, unfortunately.' His grin was boyish. 'Cupboard love, I suppose. As Nick says, no animal is going to go out and scrounge for its own fodder when it can get it without any effort at all by sticking around here. He has a point. If I stopped feeding him he might take up a natural life style.'

'If you've had him since he was a baby this *is* his natural life style,' she said. 'If you stopped feeding him he'd probably starve to death. Nick doesn't have to be right.' She caught his quick glance and lightened her tone. 'Only don't tell him I said so, will you, male pride being what it is!' She got to her feet with a certain abruptness. 'We really must go.'

'The car's on the road,' said Leo. 'We can pick Jenny up on the way round.' There was a slight hesitation before he added, 'I'm glad you called, Tara. Just sorry I wasn't more prepared. I'll have the penholder packed up ready for when you want it.'

When she did come to collect it she would have to make

sure she came alone, Tara realised. It wouldn't do for Jenny to know where the present had come from. She was also going to have to think up some plausible story for Nick should he ask how she had known his birthday was due in time to organise a present. The whole affair was fast getting out of hand, but what else could she do? She would have felt terrible sitting there on Thursday morning empty-handed while Jenny and her grandmother handed over their presents. Nick should have warned her before they left Panama, or at least while they were passing through the main island on the way here. Yet she supposed in all fairness that he wouldn't have thought of it.

If it came to that she had to acknowledge that she was going to so much trouble as much for her own benefit as his. Nick probably couldn't care less whether she gave him a present or not. Hers was the pride at stake.

CHAPTER ELEVEN

LEO dropped them off at the bottom of the drive, declining Tara's invitation to come in with them.

'I've got some paperwork to catch up on,' he said. 'We're shipping tomorrow, so that means I'll be down at the wharf most of the day.'

'Oh, can we go and watch, Tara?' asked Jenny on an eager note. 'I like seeing the cranes working.'

'I expect so,' she agreed. 'We can get Tamu to take us down. That is if we won't be in the way?' looking back at Leo with a smile.

He smiled back and shook his head. 'You won't be in the way. Everybody turns up for the occasion. Nick will probably want to bring you in himself.'

Tara had reservations on that score, but she kept them to herself. 'Well, we'll see anyway. 'Bye, Leo. And thanks for everything.'

'Glad I was able to help.' To her relief he left it at that. 'Be seeing you, Jenny. Come and visit Iggy again soon.'

'I wish I had a pet iguana,' Jenny said wistfully on the way up to the house. 'I wonder if Mr McKearn could find another baby one which needs looking after.'

'I don't think your father would be very keen on the idea,' Tara said with some reluctance. 'What you really need is a puppy or a kitten if you want a pet of your own. Or what about a pony? Can you ride at all?'

'Not very much. Daddy used to have two horses of his own when I was little, but he got rid of them when Uncle John started being ill because he didn't have time to exercise them properly any more. I don't think he'd want me to

147

have a pony. He'd say I wouldn't look after it properly.'

Damn Nick for an unfeeling brute! Tara thought in quick anger. Aloud she said reasonably, 'Well, a puppy might be the better idea. I haven't seen any dogs on the island.'

'There are a few. Sometimes they get left behind from the ships.' A spark of interest had come into Jenny's eyes. 'Do you think we might find one that's going to have pups?'

'I'm sure we would, but I was thinking more of a pedigree animal—say a spaniel or a labrador, although it might be difficult getting hold of either of those breeds in this part of the world. Your father would know more about it.'

'He won't say yes,' Jenny said flatly, the spark fading. 'I know he won't.'

It was wrong of her, and Tara knew it, but she said it anyway. 'He will, I promise, though it may take a little time to get here depending on where it has to come from.'

'I don't care how long it takes if I know I can look forward to it.' There was doubt still in the grey-blue eyes, but mingled now with hope. 'When will you ask him? Tonight?'

'Supposing we wait till Thursday,' Tara suggested on a light note. 'He can't say no on his birthday!'

Jenny didn't look particularly convinced. 'All right,' she agreed with a faint sigh. 'We'll wait till Thursday.'

Nick came out of the house as they approached, pausing beside one of the pillars to regard the two of them with unsmiling features. He was already changed into brown slacks and matching shirt with a red scarf tucked into the open neckline. He looked both dark and dangerous.

'What happened?' he demanded. 'You left here at two and it's gone half past five!'

'Two-thirty, to be exact,' Tara said levelly. 'It took longer than I'd allowed for to walk back. We called at Leo's place and he gave us a lift. He wouldn't come in.'

'Hardly surprising. He'd consider it a bit late for casual callers.' Nick's eyes went to the small figure of his daughter at Tara's side. 'Liah has your tea ready for you. Better go and tidy up before you eat. And do something with your hair. It looks like a young haystack!'

Whether the remark was intended to be humorous or not, Jenny took it that way. Her laugh was quick and happy. 'I've been playing with Iggy,' she said. 'He kept pulling it with his claws.'

Nick waited until she had skipped on ahead into the house before saying tautly, 'I told Leo to get rid of that creature. There's no knowing what it might be carrying.'

'Oh, but surely if it's clean and well looked after there can't be much wrong with it,' Tara protested. 'I think he'd feel lost without it around the place now. I thought it a rather attractive little animal.'

'You might change your mind when it's fully grown. They can reach over three feet in length. Some house pet!'

There was an opening in there for a mention of Jenny's needs, but she didn't take it. Nick's mood was unpredictable, his concern over their non-return too close to anger to risk any further clash of opinion. She said instead, 'Leo mentioned that you'd be shipping out tomorrow. Do you mind if Jenny and I come down to watch?'

His shrug was indifferent. 'Why should I mind? I'll run you down in the morning and bring you back before lunch.'

'Couldn't we take a picnic out with us?' Tara tried hard to sound natural about it. 'Jenny would love it.'

'I'm sure she would,' he said dryly, 'but there won't be time.'

'There never is,' she said, and walked on into the house, chin held high.

He caught her up halfway across the hall, taking her by an arm and bringing her to a stop. His expression was anything but reassuring.

'There are one or two things it's high time you learned,' he said harshly. 'I'm running a business here, not a holiday camp. And talking of time, you're spending a darn sight too much of it on Jenny as it is!'

Anger made her reckless. 'Isn't that what you hired me for?'

His mouth snapped into one straight frightening line, his fingers digging into the soft flesh of her upper arm. Without speaking, he turned her about and pushed her ahead of him into the library, closing the door behind him to regard her with cold hard eyes.

'Just say that again.'

'Nick, I'm sorry.' Her voice shook, as much in self-disgust as fear of what he might do. 'That was a rotten crack to make!'

'You're telling me?' His control alone was unnerving. 'God, you go all out for reprisals, don't you! I'd like to shake you rigid!'

'I said I was sorry!'

'And that's supposed to make everything hunky-dory again, I suppose.'

'No.' Her temper died as swiftly as it had flared, her face registering distress. 'No, of course it doesn't. I—I didn't stop to consider what I was saying. Will you believe that, Nick? I honestly am sorry.'

'So am I.' He let her go, flexing his fingers as he moved past her to the desk by the window. There were cigarettes in an onyx box on top of it. He took one out and put it between his lips, thumbing a lighter into flames with a click which sounded savage in the quietness of the room and drawing on the smoke in a way totally alien to the other odd occasions when she had seen him with a cigarette. When he finally looked her way again it was with scarcely less hardness than before. 'I can understand now why men murder their wives!'

150

Tara leaned against the door to conceal the trembling in her limbs, head bent. 'Some of the things you've said to me mightn't stand too much mulling over,' she murmured thickly. 'There are faults on both sides.'

'I wouldn't deny it. The biggest mine for failing to make allowances for the gap between us.'

'You mean in age?' She paused. 'Twelve years isn't that much, it is?'

'In some cases it wouldn't make a great deal of difference, true. In ours it appears to be unbridgeable.' He paused, eyeing the smouldering end of the cigarette with disfavour. 'You need a father more than you need a husband, and that's not a role I find easy to play—as you've already gathered.'

'That's not true!'

'No?' He studied her for a long moment, taking in the tousled hair and flushed unhappy face, moving down with a calm deliberation over her jean-clad figure to stop at the rolled knees. 'You don't look all that much older than Jenny right now. Is it any real wonder I find it hard sometimes to separate my reactions?'

Her throat hurt. 'Was I any different before you decided to marry me?'

'I believed so. You said what you thought then too, but without the viciousness. Maybe that's something I've taught you. I don't pretend to be a holy Joe.' He paused again, expression unreadable, said softly, 'Just why did you agree to marry me, Tara?'

Because I was in love with you, she wanted to say; except that she knew it wasn't true. She hadn't loved this man, she had loved a product of her own imagination: the kind of man she had wanted him to be. For the first time she was able to see it straight. But it was this man who was her husband; this man who had held her in his arms and possessed her wholly and completely as a woman. If she felt

151

anything for him at all it was in a way she couldn't yet begin to define with any certainty. All she was sure of was that he had the power to hurt her as nothing or no one had hurt her before.

'I don't know,' she said without emotion. 'Security, perhaps.'

'Nothing else?'

Blue eyes met grey briefly, and a faint colour tinged her cheeks again. 'Why bother to ask when you already know the answer to that? Elementary, didn't you say the other night?'

'Did I?' He sounded wry. 'Not very tactful of me, was it?'

'But more than true, I'm sure. You knew the very first time you kissed me that you could make me ... want you that way. I suppose men always know these things.'

'By course of experience, you mean?' He shrugged. 'I wouldn't deny having sown a few wild oats in my time. You object?'

She shook her head, not looking at him. 'I can accept that sort of experience.'

'But not a previous wife.' His tone had gone flat. It was a moment or two before he spoke again. 'If I told you about Helen do you think it would make any real difference? We'd still be the same people with the same problems.'

'But surely a little closer in understanding. You must have loved her very much.'

His lips twisted. 'Certainly more than she felt for me. She was drowned running away with another man. Does that supply any answers?'

'It might.' She was choosing her words with care. 'You said Jenny was like her.'

'In more ways than one, petulant, self-willed; sulking when she can't have her own way.'

'Jenny doesn't sulk. She just retreats inside herself when she's hurt or upset.'

152

Nick's smile was faint. 'You seem to have fathomed more about her in the short time you've been here than I've managed to do in nine years.'

'According to you I'm little more than a kid myself. Maybe that's why.'

'Don't put words into my mouth. I didn't say in everything.' His mood had changed again, returning to hardness. 'This is doing no good for either of us. Forget it.'

'Nick ...' it was out before she could consider the wisdom of putting it into words ... 'Jenny could only be *your* child. There can't be any doubt in your mind about that.'

The lean features had gone blank. When he spoke it was in measured tones. 'Nothing I've told you could possibly have put that idea in your head.'

'Nothing you've actually said, no.' Anna had to be kept out of it, she thought desperately. He must never know just how much his mother had told her already about his first marriage. 'But it's there in your eyes when you look at her —even just now when you talked about her. It clicked into place when you mentioned this other man.'

There were flaws in the explanation; she could see them from here. From the narrowing of his eyes he saw them too. She jumped in again quickly before he could comment. 'Anyone can see the resemblance between you. I saw it that very first time I met her.'

'So you said at the time.' He was still eyeing her in that calculating manner as though trying to work something out. 'Any other observations to make while we're about it? It seems to be the season for it.'

'No.' She came away from the door, aware of already having said too much. 'You were right the first time. It isn't any use. We were mistaken to ever think it might be.'

'Then it's a mistake we're going to have to live with,' he said. 'One way or another.' The cigarette was crushed into the tray. 'Hadn't you better go and change?'

Tara went without argument. There was little point in staying. All they'd done was make things worse than before. One thing was certain—she would not share this mockery of a marriage with Olivia in any shape or form. If necessary she would take a leaf out of Helen's book and leave him. There was an aching emptiness in that thought.

It was a long evening, made longer by an unusual oppressiveness in the atmosphere. Tara played Scrabble with Jenny after an early dinner, and was taken aback when Nick consented to join them for a game at Jenny's request.

'Good exercise,' he said in answer to her unspoken question. His smile was mocking. 'Finding the right words, I mean. Most of us need practice in that.'

He needed little, winning two games outright and declining to play off a third against his daughter.

'You're just looking for an excuse to stay up,' he said, and she grinned back at him.

'I know. Gran says you hated going to bed when you were my age too.'

'Gran says a sight too much,' he responded on a note which held a faint underlying edge. 'Scoot, kiddy!'

'Okay.' Jenny went resignedly to the door. 'You won't forget about tomorrow, will you?'

'I won't.' The pause was brief. 'How would you like to go up to Tubai Bay after you've seen the loading? I daresay I could find a couple of hours round midday.'

'Oh yes!' The tone was eager, eyes wide and blissful. 'Tara and Gran too?'

'Not me, thanks,' Anna declined smilingly. 'If I want a beach we have a perfectly good one right here. It's too hot to go driving around in the middle of the day at my age. With you all out of the way I can flake out on the veranda and have a good read.'

She waited until Jenny had finally taken her leave before

looking at her son. 'That was a nice gesture, Nick.'

'Tara's idea,' he responded without turning his head. 'She thinks I neglect the child.' He found Tara's eyes, his own veiled. 'Feel like a walk?'

She was cautious in answering, not sure of his mood. 'I wouldn't mind.'

'Don't hurry back,' Anna said comfortably. 'I'm going to play some Bach. Nick can't stand him,' she added for Tara's benefit. 'Especially the choral stuff. I really must get some stereo equipment in my own room.'

'Along with some soundproofing, I hope.' The edge was still there, faint but unmistakable. If Anna noted it herself she seemed content to ignore it.

The night was moonless, the stars packed close in a sky which had depth in its blackness. They took the path which led down through the banana and peach trees beyond the rear lawns, coming out at length above the rocky little headland that formed the southern limits of the bay. Nick had said little since leaving the house, touching her only when he deemed it necessary to guide her footsteps over the rougher bits.

'I haven't been this way before,' Tara said when he paused to light a cigarette. He was smoking more than she had ever seen him do to date. Normally it was just the odd cheroot in the evening. 'How big is the island altogether?'

'Roughly about the same size as your Isle of Wight—if you know it.'

'I've spent a couple of holidays there way back.'

'So long ago?' on an ironical note. 'Your parents take you?'

'The first time. I went with a girl friend when I was sixteen.'

'Meet any nice boys?'

'One.' She smiled, remembering. 'He was eighteen, and so sophisticated. He and his friend took Sheila and me out to supper in a rather posh restaurant one night. When the waiter poured him the wine to taste he said it was corked and to change it. From where I was sitting I could see the waiter behind the screen in front of the kitchen doors forcing the cork back into the bottle. He brought the same bottle back with the corkscrew already in it to hide the hole. I suffered total disillusionment when Jeremy didn't even realise he'd been tricked.'

Nick shrugged. 'Not tricked so much as pandered to. He was lucky. Some might not have taken the trouble.' There was a pause before he added, 'I gather that finished the romance forthwith?'

'So far as it had gone. At sixteen everything had to be perfect.'

'I wouldn't have said you'd changed all that much. If something doesn't come up to expectations you still want to scrap it out of hand.'

'If you're talking about us it isn't quite the same thing, is it?' Her voice was low. 'We didn't start out with any illusions, just a hope which hasn't been fulfilled.'

'It's barely had time—or opportunity. We've lived more like brother and sister than man and wife since we came to Silverwood.'

She said thickly, 'Whose fault is that?'

He gave her an oblique glance. 'You're asking me why I haven't done something about that promise I made you? Is that what you want; a husband who leaves you no alternative!' His tone had hardened again. 'Did it ever occur to you that a man might look for a little more than mere availability?'

'You said I ... responded.'

'Oh, yes, you do that all right,' with irony. 'What you never do is initiate. If you want me to make love to you I expect you to show it.'

'To be all woman, you mean?' Her jaw felt rigid. 'I'm

sorry if I lack the kind of experience you're used to!'

'For God's sake stop it!' The cigarette was crushed between finger and thumb and tossed viciously over the edge of the low cliff a few feet away. Hands reached out for her, jerking her towards him and holding her there in front of him. 'Do I have to draw you a diagram to get what I'm trying to say through to you?' He gazed down at her, mouth thinning. 'Maybe I do at that. All right, so we'll start from scratch. Kiss me.'

She stared at him with eyes wide and dark. 'Nick, I . . .'

'Don't talk—act.' He took her hands and put them on his shoulders, resting his own either side of her waist. His mouth was implacable. 'Either you make some effort towards this relationship of ours or you accept the only other alternative I'm going to feel in the mood for tonight!'

Her voice felt trapped in her throat. 'There has to be more than this, Nick—for any kind of start!'

'It appears to be all we have. Therefore we'll make it do.' There was no softening of his features in the cold starry light. 'Are you going to meet me halfway, Tara, or shall I start teaching you what brutes men really can be!'

'You'll make me hate you either way,' she said huskily. 'Don't you mind *that*?'

'No. At least it's positive.' Hands bruising he brought her up on her toes. 'I said kiss me!'

She did with stiff lips, refusing to submit herself wholly to the threat yet conscious at the same time of his power to stir her. When she moved back away from him he didn't try to stop her, his smile sardonic as he studied her face.

'You'll learn. You're going to have to learn if you want to keep me out of Olivia's bed—and that's what bothers you most, isn't it?'

'If you'd let me go she could have you and welcome,' she said through her teeth. 'Someone like her deserves no better!'

'Careful, darling, you're retrogressing.' Eyes glinting, he put an arm across her shoulders and turned her in the direction from which they had come. 'This marriage of ours might not be exactly perfect, but I've a feeling it's going to take on an added zest from now on. You've more about you when you're spitting fire; you always did have. I should have realised before what was needed.'

'Swine!' she choked, and pulled free of him as his hard laugh rang out, to stumble blindly on ahead up the path.

It was inevitable that she should fall, of course. It was too dark amid the trees to see where she was going. Nick came up as she pushed herself on to her knees, drawing her to her feet and proffering a handkerchief with a dry little smile as she dashed an angry tear from the corner of her eyes with the back of her hand.

'Come on now,' he said. 'It's hardly as bad as that. We've shared the same experience before. The only difference is going to be in attitude—yours to me. You might even come to disregard obligations. Remember the oracle: 'tis better to give than to receive!'

'Nick, don't be like this,' she begged, sinking pride for the moment. 'What good will it do?'

'Quite a lot—for me.' He was unmoved. 'I've tried the treading softly bit; now it's time to progress. If we don't have anything else we'll build on basic attraction. And don't start trying to deny that too,' as she made to speak. 'Like you said earlier, I'm capable of recognising that much. Let's get back to the house.'

She went with him because there was nowhere else to go, biting back any further protests in the knowledge of their uselessness. What he had issued her with was an ultimatum, no more no less: she went along with what he demanded of her or he turned to Olivia for solace. If she were able to believe that anything real and true and lasting might grow from any of this it would be different, but Nick wasn't capable of any depth of emotion. Not now. Helen had used up what vulnerability he had ever possessed.

Tara slanted a glance at him walking at her side, dark and ruthless and inescapable. What he wanted from her was total commitment to a marriage which at its best could never give her all *she* needed from it. Or was it simply that she wanted too much? Did any marriage achieve an equal balance, if it came to that, or was one partner always fated to care more deeply than the other? If the latter were so then perhaps she should learn to accept it, because hers would be that role, there was nothing surer. Much as she had tried to deny it, she already cared too much.

The house was quiet when they went in, the drawing room lights turned low, Anna's chair vacated. Seeing the time, Tara could scarcely credit that almost two hours had passed since they had left her here. She would have retired for the night by now. She always went at ten-thirty.

Nick made no comment on his mother's absence, just went over and closed the lid of the record deck, then turned to the cabinet close by.

'Do you want a drink?' he asked.

Tara shook her head. Alcohol was no answer. She had to deal with this situation on her own. 'I think I'll go on up,' she said with what calmness she could muster.

'Right.' He didn't look at her. 'I won't be long.'

There was an odd lack of emotionalism in her as she performed the nightly ritual which preceded sleep. Only when she donned the blue wrap did the coldness begin to give way a little before the memories it evoked.

Sitting down in front of the dressing table mirror to brush her hair, she was aware of an added intensity in the blue of the eyes gazing back at her, of a quivering expectancy growing slowly within her. It seemed an age since Nick had shown any real desire for her, even of the physical kind. If tonight she had to prove to him that she felt it too

159

then surely it wasn't such a terrible price to pay? Men were such physical creatures. To reach their hearts one must obviously first appeal to the senses. If she wanted Nick to love her the way she loved him then she must be prepared to use what aids Nature had seen fit to provide her with, and close her mind to any underlying calculation.

He came in while she was still sitting there with the brush in her hand, his eyes meeting hers for just a moment as he crossed behind her to take off his jacket and sling it over a chair. Heart beating fast and hard, she watched him loosen his tie and pull it free of the collar, saw the lean brown hand unfasten the first three buttons of his shirt.

With fingers gone nerveless, she put down the brush as he came slowly over to where she sat, recognising the moment yet still not certain how to react to it. Only when he laid his hand on her shoulder did her instincts come to life, inclining her head so that her cheek brushed his warm, firm skin. She saw his face subtly change expression, his eyes acquire a deeper spark. When he lifted her and turned her into his arms she went without reservation, her face uptilted to meet his lips.

CHAPTER TWELVE

THEY left the house for Ruru shortly after nine-thirty, reaching the waterfront to find the big cargo vessel already docked and loading well in hand. Nick left Tara and Jenny in the wharf office where Leo was dealing with the paperwork involved in the transaction, saying that from there they could see all there was to be seen without getting in the way of the humming activity outside.

'I'll be back about eleven-thirty,' he said from the doorway. The smile he gave Tara was brief but heartwarming.

'I hope we're not going to put you off your figuring,' she said in some concern to Leo after Nick had gone out to check on proceedings so far. 'I'm sure we could find a safe corner outside.'

'No, not at all,' he hastened to assure her. 'Anyway, Nick said you were to stay here until ...' He paused, and smiled one of his endearingly wry little smiles. 'Sorry. It's hardly up to me to point out what Nick said to his own wife. It just becomes a matter of habit to regard his word as rather the law round here. I mean, everyone does. Not that he's always laying it down, of course.'

'You don't have to explain, Leo,' Tara said with some amusement. 'I can quite appreciate your point. Having dumped us here he'll expect to find us waiting for him here at eleven-thirty, but providing we don't get in the way there's nothing to stop us stepping outside now and then.' She looked round and wrinkled her nose. 'It's too stuffy in here anyway. Couldn't you at least have a fan rigged up?'

'Not unless I can find some youngster willing to spend time waving a palm frond over me,' he returned without

161

rancour. 'Can't waste generator power on that kind of luxury.'

Jenny was standing in the open doorway surveying the scene along the busy wharf. Now she said plaintively, 'It's going to be boring if we do have to stay here. Can we really go outside for a while, Tara?'

With the ball landed fairly and squarely in her court, she found herself hesitating. There could be no harm in it providing they were careful, and she doubted if Nick had really intended them to stick so close. Now, less than ever, did she want to get across him in any way. Not when they were just beginning to gain some understanding of one another. There had been a difference in Nick this morning; a lowering of the barriers in a sense which had reminded her of their first days together before they reached Mataleta. They might be a long way still from achieving all she hoped for, but their present harmony was a good start. She wanted it to last.

'I'll tell you what,' she said. 'Sit and watch from the doorstep for now and we'll go out when they've finished clearing this nearest warehouse. That way the trundling about will be well ahead of us.'

'A safe middle course,' Leo agreed with a gentle mockery which surprised her. He waited until Jenny had complied with the suggestion before adding on a slight note of hesitation, 'When will you be picking up Nick's present, do you think?'

That matter was still a source of worry to Tara, but there seemed no adequate alternative. She must have something to give to Nick. She simply must! And he would like the pen stand, she was sure of that. He couldn't fail to like it.

'Tomorrow,' she said. 'Only I'm not sure just when I'll be able to manage it. Do you think you could leave it in Kim's care so that I can pop over when I can?'

'I think a better idea might be if I brought it over in the

162

car during the evening and you slipped out to take it from me. That way you at least stand a chance of getting it into the house undetected.' Leo laughed suddenly. 'We sound like a couple of conspirators, don't we!'

They were precisely that, she thought with wry acceptance, yet the suggestion was a more sensible one than her own. 'All right,' she agreed. 'Thanks, Leo. Can you make it around nine-thirty if possible?'

'Will do. I'll park at the bottom of the drive.'

And she would have to find an excuse to get her out of the way of the others for at least fifteen minutes. It wasn't going to be easy, but then nothing worthwhile ever was.

'You ought to find yourself a wife, Leo,' she said on impulse. 'You really would make some girl a wonderfully thoughtful husband!'

'There's more to marriage than thoughtfulness.' There was an odd note in his voice and he avoided her eyes. 'I'd need to be in love with a girl before I could start thinking along those lines—and she with me.'

'And there's no one you feel like that about? Back home, I mean.'

'Not back home, no.' He seemed to be speaking with some care for what he said. 'I do have a rather high regard for one of the teachers at the school here in Ruru. Her name is Leyita. She was born on the island but proved herself so bright Nick financed an outside education for her. She came back here about the same time I started as manager.'

'Was that a condition Nick made?' Tara asked, and was relieved when he shook his head.

'No, she never wanted anything else but to come back and put what she'd learned to use in the school right here. Neither will she ever want to leave Mataleta.'

'Whereas you very likely will one day.'

It was a moment before he answered that one. 'It's

possible. Life has a way of catching up on one.'

'Which is more than can be said for you with those invoices,' came Nick's dry tones from the doorway. 'I thought Jenny was supposed to be in your care, Tara?'

She had started guiltily, seeing the empty step for the first time. 'Oh, heavens! Where is she?'

'I've put her on an empty packing case in a corner and told her to stay there.' The glance he rested on the younger man's bent head held a curious quality. 'I think Leo can do without any more distractions. Come and say hallo to the *Ballantyre*'s skipper—he was a friend of Dan Anders.'

Tara waited until they were outside and out of earshot before saying tentatively, 'You know, it was entirely my fault if Leo was falling down on the job back there.'

'So I gathered.' He had his hands in his pockets, expression unrevealing. 'I shouldn't have left you with him in the first place.'

There was nothing to say to that. Better to let it go anyway. Nick obviously hadn't liked finding the two of them talking the way they had been. Jealousy? No, not exactly, she decided. More possessiveness. Jealousy suggested insecurity, and Nick was hardly that.

The ship's captain was called Larson; a man about Dan Anders' age and not unlike him in appearance.

'Glad everything turned out okay for you folk, at any rate,' he said gruffly when Tara proffered her sincere regrets over the other man's death. 'It was the way Dan would have wanted to go. Lived for the sea since he was a boy.' He looked across the untidy cabin to where Nick stood at the port looking out on the wharf. 'Leave it alone, man. The job'll get done in time. We're well inside schedule. How about a drink? Got some malt Scotch goes down like velvet!' His eyes came back to Tara as if in sudden recollection of her sex and status. 'Plenty of coffee going in the galley if you'd fancy some?'

She smiled back at him. 'I'd love some.'

While the coffee was coming the two men sampled the whisky, leaving Tara to wonder at the constitutions which could accept, even enjoy, hard liquor at ten-forty-five in the morning with the heat already somewhere in the eighties. Last night's oppressiveness had not so much lifted as changed character. There was a brooding stillness in the atmosphere. Nick had made no comment on it coming down here earlier, but she had seen his glances go more than once to the cloudless blue sky as if in calculation. If there was a storm coming he must have decided it would not reach them for some time yet, as he had made no attempt to cancel arrangements for their picnic.

They took their leave of Captain Larson promptly on the half hour, and went to find Jenny. She was still sitting where Nick had put her, though whether she had been there the whole time between was anyone's guess.

It wasn't until they were in the car and heading away from the waterfront that he said levelly, 'Afraid we're going to have to leave Tubai for another day. There isn't going to be time. I thought we might take our picnic up on Taki Hill. It's not too far from the house.'

'Daddy, you *promised*!' Jenny's voice was accusing. 'You can't break a promise!'

His lips had straightened. 'There are times when we all have to. That's something you're going to have to learn one day, and now's as good a time as any. It's either Taki or straight back home. Which do you prefer?'

Tara crossed her fingers as her stepdaughter hesitated, seeing the rebellious expression cross the young face and sympathising with her obvious first impulse. She drew a breath of relief when Jenny finally opened her mouth.

'We'll go to Taki, then,' she said, and looked out of the window with set, unsmiling features.

They were almost within reach of Silverwood before

Nick took one of the narrow lanes, little more than tracks, rising into the backbone of hills which split the island down the centre. Huge clumps of fern smothered the ground beneath the trees to either hand, giving way occasionally to bright patches of the same profusely flowering creeper that graced the pillars along Silverwood's frontage. There were glimpses of the sea, vast and blue and shimmering, curling white where it met the land. And lofting over all the hazy shape of the volcano from which the island took its name, the summit depressed as though by a thumb plunged in and withdrawn.

Jenny cheered up again soon enough once they reached the natural, open amphitheatre scooped out of the hillside by past eons of wind and storm, vanishing to explore as soon as she had eaten her fill from the overloaded basket Tem Gan had packed for them.

'Wouldn't it be possible to let her go to one of the island schools at least a part of the time?' Tara asked impulsively. 'I realise standards must be geared to a certain level, but some subjects are universal.'

Nick was a moment answering. 'You were the one who scotched the idea of her needing school. Finding the alternative too much for you?'

'I was thinking of the limitations. Academically, I think we can manage for another year or so, following the syllabus Miss Cartwright worked out for her. But she does need companionship. Did you see the way she responded to the other children on the beach that night?' The mention of that particular event brought back other disturbing memories. She hurried on. 'I was talking to one of the teachers on the beach yesterday. He was saying how short they are of staff. Perhaps Jenny and I could both benefit from a few sessions down there.'

'You're not working in any school,' he said flatly. 'The islanders wouldn't appreciate it any more than I would.

And Jenny's going there could only cause disruption too.'

'Because of her standing as your daughter?'

'Partly. Whether you like it or not, the Bryants are held in rather high esteem by these people as a class apart. Feudalism to a certain extent, maybe, but there's little I can do about it. It's the way they themselves prefer things. It's only been in my father's time that they've begun acknowledging an outside world at all. Even now few of them leave here for good.'

'Then why bother educating them at all?' She shook her head as the possible interpretation of that question struck her. 'I'm not criticising, Nick, just genuinely curious. If they're so content with their lot right here on Mataleta it seems a waste of time to teach them things which will only be of use to them away from it.'

'That was the initial view. My father was able to persuade them that their children were entitled to an opportunity to decide for themselves when the time came.'

'Wasn't that risking a lot? He could eventually have finished up with no work force to draw on at all.'

'Very unlikely. The majority can't imagine any life better than this no matter what they learn. Still no reason why they should be denied the knowledge because only a handful make full use of it.'

'Like Leyita, for instance?'

He slanted a glance. 'Who told you about her?'

'Leo. We were talking about her when you came to fetch me.'

There was no visible reaction, but she was almost certain he had experienced one. 'Wasn't aware he knew her. She's a very dedicated girl, more serious minded than the average. The Polynesian would rather play any day than work.'

Tara laughed. 'Wouldn't we all!'

'Not with quite the same attitude to life.'

'But they all seem willing enough to work too.'

'Just enough to provide the essentials. Luckily there are enough of them to make constant change-overs a feasible operation. A man works until he considers he's made his and his family's keep for a few days, then he stands down and another takes over. It's a scheme they devised themselves to keep everybody happy and the island productive at one and the same time. As they grow a lot of their own produce they don't need much extra, apart from clothing.'

'Which in this climate hardly means a large wardrobe.' Tara was lying back against a tussock of grass, eyes shielded from the brassy glare of the sun. 'It sounds like Utopia.'

'Hardly that. There's no such thing as perfect harmony where the human race is concerned. We're not made that way. There's as much squabbling over petty jealousies here as anywhere else.' Mockery infiltrated his voice. 'Usually over women. Something to do with the French blood in their ancestry, perhaps.'

The hand stayed over her eyes. 'It's true then that the Frenchman thinks more about love than any others?'

'I wouldn't say he thinks more about it, just makes more time for the pursual of it.'

She removed the shielding hand as his shadow fell across her, looking up into the strong dark features with a mingling of emotions. He was smiling faintly. 'You'd rather I were French?'

She shook her head, not trusting her voice, saw his eyes move down to her mouth and linger there and managed a husky appeal, 'Jenny might come back, Nick.'

'And you think it would shock her to see me kissing you?' with satire. 'Even a child of nine must be aware that adults exchange that kind of greeting from time to time.'

'But not between the two of us. At least not yet.' She couldn't get up because of the way he was leaning over her, and there was a distinct disadvantage to arguing a point like this one from such a position, yet she had to try to make him see it. 'Jenny is just beginning to accept me as a friend. If I arouse her jealousy she'll hate me again.'

'Jealousy!' Nick pressed himself abruptly upright. 'Good God, you're talking about a kid, not another woman!'

'She's still female.' The pause was brief, the beating of her heart loud in her ears. 'And she loves you, Nick, even if you don't love her back.'

She had hoped he would deny the charge, but he didn't. There was impatience in the line of his mouth. 'I'm just about up to here with all this psychology! You're my wife —and the sooner Jenny realises it the better!'

'But she's your child. Surely that ...'

'She's not my child.' The words were torn from him through clamped teeth. 'Can't you get it through your head? She never was *mine*!'

The sudden gust of hot wind came almost simultaneously with Tara's glimpse of the small figure standing stock still on the lip of rock some yards beyond Nick's broad shoulders. How long Jenny had been there she had no way of knowing. Nor was it possible to tell from the expressionless little face just how much she might have overheard. There wasn't even time to worry about it right now, for Nick had sprung to his feet with an air of urgency.

'Get in the car,' he ordered as the wind came again with a strength that lifted the picnic basket lid and banged it back on to the ground. 'I'll collect the things.' He turned then and saw Jenny, but registered no surprise or shock. 'Both of you, into the car and be quick about it!'

Tara obeyed without question, grabbing Jenny in passing and hurrying her over to the Range Rover. Safely installed, she watched Nick diving towards them through a world filled with flying debris whirled in crazy spirals by the gusts already merging into one continuous blow. It was all the more terrifying that something like this could drop on them out of a clear sky and in two minutes wreak such havoc.

The palms below were a frenzy of green, the dust eddying skywards from the road in yellow clouds. Nick was hard put to hold the door as he tossed basket and rug into the back and climbed into the driving seat. The Rover was rocking like a boat in a rough sea.

'I should have had more sense than to bring you up here,' he clipped when he had the car moving. 'I knew this was coming, but I calculated we had time enough to make it back before it struck.'

So that was why he had refused to take them to Tubai. Tara wished he had only said so at the time. She took a glance at Jenny in the back seat, but the child's face was averted towards the window, her whole attention riveted on the devastation outside. A tree fell with a crash just short of the road, uprooted as if it were as light as a matchstick. The sea which such a short time before had been so tranquil now rose in gigantic chaos, splintered with white as far as eye could see. There was nothing out there, fortunately. The islanders too would have recognised the signs. She thought of the *Ballantyre* down at the wharf, remembering the Captain's words that morning. They hadn't had time to complete the loading after all, and they certainly wouldn't be able to continue in this.

'How long is it likely to last?' she shouted above the howling, hanging on like grim death to the back of the seat as Nick fought to keep the vehicle upright.

'It's in the lap of the gods,' he shouted back. 'A few hours, or a couple of days. You'll be safe enough at the house.'

If they ever reached it. Tara set her teeth against the fear swamping her and concentrated on keeping her seat. Jenny hadn't uttered a word since getting into the car, but she didn't appear to be terror-stricken. She was probably accustomed to such vagaries of weather—either that or too wrapped up in her own personal horror to register what was going on out there at all. Tara hoped against hope that she hadn't heard what Nick had said. That would be too cruel. How could a child her age be expected to understand the feelings of a man who had lived with that kind of doubt for nine years? If only she could find some way of convincing him how wrong he was about Jenny. But how? He was never going to believe it because he didn't want to believe it; because by accepting Helen's child as his he would be robbing himself of the main reason for despising her memory.

That they made Silverwood at all was a wonder, that they made it without undue mishap next thing to a miracle. Anna waited for them in the hall, windows shuttered and barred, everything movable brought in from the porch.

'You're not going out again in this?' she exclaimed in dismay when Nick turned back to the door after seeing Tara and Jenny safely inside.

'I've got to get to the wharf while it's still possible to move at all,' he said. 'It's going to take all hands to keep that ship tied down.'

'You mean it might get worse than this?' queried Tara in dry-throated apprehension, and he glanced her way with a hand already on the rattling door.

'There's every chance. Don't go out again, for *any* reason. Do you hear? I'll be back when I can.'

Tamu and one of the other men sprang to hold the door as he went out, slamming it to again and locking it. In here the howl was muted but no less fear-striking. It was only just possible to hear the car start up and move off.

'Don't worry, Nick knows what he's doing,' Anna said reassuringly, though without great conviction. 'How far away were you when it started?'

'Taki Hill.' As much for Jenny's benefit as her grandmother's she added, 'Nick decided it wouldn't be worth risking Tubai when he realised this was on its way, though how he could tell I can't imagine.'

'It's a feeling in the air as much as anything else. As a matter of fact, I half expected him to cancel the whole thing this morning.'

'I suppose he didn't want to disappoint Jenny altogether.' Tara cast a worried glance in the child's direction as she wandered off into the library with hands stuck disconsolately into her jeans pockets. 'Does this kind of thing bother her at all?'

'Not that I've noticed.' Anna stirred restlessly. 'We can't hang about here. Come and have some tea. It's far too early, but what of it?'

True to Nick's prediction the gale force increased as night fell, crashing tiles from the roof and hammering the shutters against their confining bars. Despite the noise, Jenny took herself off to bed at the normal time, still without having strung more than a few odd words together since returning to the house. There was little Tara could do to comfort her without knowing just how much she had overheard. There was still a chance that her present diffidence had sprung from just the sight of the two of them together and so absorbed they had never even noticed her. If so she would no doubt get over it. Tara could only hope that was all.

It was ridiculous to expect Nick back that night, of course, but she found herself waiting for him nevertheless, her nerves leaping to every new sound in the hope of its somehow being the car. Neither she nor Anna felt like going to bed. Sleep would just about be impossible anyway. They sat up listening to music and reading by the flickering light supply, with Anna expressing the fervent desire that the wind-driven generator would not cut out on them altogether.

When the gale did finally die in the early hours of the

morning it did so as suddenly as it had sprung into being, the silence like that of the grave. The two women eased themselves out of the chairs in which they had sat through the worst and went by common consent to take a look outside. Even in moonlight the devastation was appalling. Tara could take heart only from Anna's apparent lack of concern. No doubt the damage looked worse than it really was. In any case, mopping up operations could hardly begin before daylight, and that was another couple of hours away yet.

Bed seemed the only sensible idea now that everything was quiet again. Lying in the middle of her lonely one, Tara tried not to worry too much about Nick's non-return. There would be a lot of clearing up to do at the wharf before they could finish loading the freighter, to say nothing of the township itself. Even now the little clinic would no doubt be overrun with casualties caused by flying debris and collapsing buildings. She could appreciate for the first time why all the islanders' dwellings were constructed of light materials which would inflict the least damage to person and property if blown down. They were more easily replaced too, although she didn't imagine such gales struck Mataleta all that often. After last night she hated to think what it must be like to be caught in the path of a hurricane.

It seemed an age before she finally slept.

CHAPTER THIRTEEN

IT was mid-afternoon before Nick returned. He looked tired and grimy but was able to report no serious damage. The *Ballantyre* had already sailed, so for the moment they could concentrate on setting things to rights again.

'I'll just grab a sandwich and a change of clothing,' he said. 'If the rain comes now there's going to be a lot of families without a roof over their heads. We've organised a work force to start repairs, but they're going to need constant gingering up to get them done in any reasonable time.'

'Isn't there anything I can do?' Tara asked swiftly as he made towards the stairs. 'The damage here was fairly superficial and the servants have taken care of most of it.'

His appraisal was quick and decisive. 'You could be useful at the clinic. They're run off their feet. Few bad injuries but plenty of cuts and bruises. Get somebody to tear up a few sheets for bandages while I change, will you. Supplies were getting low when I called in.'

Anna was already in the kitchen organising a meal for her son. Knowing he would refuse to wait, Tara changed it to a cold snack and asked for flasks filled with hot coffee. The sheets were dutifully torn into strips and packed ready for transportation. By the time Nick came down again she was all prepared.

It was distressing to see the uprooted trees and battle-scarred terrain on the way into town, but in this climate recovery would be swift. The township itself was not as bad as she had anticipated, and the people seemed philosophical enough about it all, many of them singing as they worked

174

on the repairs. What was a bit of a gale after all? Nobody had died, and houses could be rebuilt.

The clinic held a little more evidence of drama in the patient queue of people still waiting to get inside its doors. Tara had already met the medical staff of three, and was aware that a doctor visited the island each week. Any serious cases were despatched to one of the larger islands for treatment, although illnesses of that nature were rare on Mataleta. Only on occasions like this one did facilities prove somewhat less than adequate.

There was good order in the two wards, the concussions contained in the quietest end of the smaller one, the balance of beds given over to children and old folk less able to cope with their injuries. The young nurse in charge, who held the nominal rank of Sister, was bandaging a youth's head in the surgery while her two assistants sorted out the remaining patients in order of priority. She acknowledged Tara's arrival with deferential gratitude and willingly relinquished her present task to the fresh hands in order to examine a child with a possible broken arm.

'Some of them have waited all day before bothering to come,' she explained after Nick had departed. Her English was slow and methodical. 'My people have no love of the smell of this place.' She said something which sounded reassuring to the small boy in her own language, and patted his head before lifting him down to the floor again. 'There is no break in the bone, but he is very bruised. A fence fell on him.' Watching Tara's efforts with the bandage as she washed her hands, she added, 'You have some training yourself?'

'Just elementary first aid, I'm afraid.' Tara smiled at the youth and indicated that he could go, hoping the bandage would stay put. 'I'm not very quick.'

'But you are careful, and that is important too. At the hospital where I learned to be a nurse we were taught that

175

speed is essential only where it may save a life. At all other times a proper regulated pace must be observed. We will work well together.'

They did too, especially as it became clear that the queue of patients was dwindling without further addition. Only when they were finally clear did Tara remember the coffee still in the holdall Nick had carried in for her. She had meant to give him a couple of the flasks to take with him.

Sharing the third with the three staff, she asked the Sister if she knew where her husband would most likely be working, and was advised that the waterfront area had sustained the worst of the damage. There were protests when she proposed walking down with the other flasks, but she overrode them smilingly. It was only a short distance and it would do her good to stretch her legs, she said.

The clinic was set halfway up the hill towards the rear of the settlement, looking out over a scatter of roofs to a placid sea. There were boats out again, frail-looking outrigger canoes gliding over the sparkling water on the lookout for fish. The tall palms lofted towards a sky balmy with early evening light, still and stately and untouched by the elements. Viewing the scene, Tara could readily understand what motivated the islanders to stay all their lives in this one spot, regardless of what might befall them. She had come under Mataleta's spell herself.

She found Nick working alongside the others on repairs to the roofs of dwellings just off the waterfront, the whole party watched with great seriousness by two thumb-sucking toddlers wearing nothing but tattered shorts. He came down the roughly constructed ladder when he spotted her approaching, brows contracted a little.

'I said I'd pick you up at the clinic before dark.'

'I know, but we'd finished dealing with patients for the time being, so I thought you might appreciate some coffee,' she said. 'It should still be hot.'

'I just had some, but leave it anyway. It will come in.' He sounded preoccupied. 'As a matter of fact, I was going to tell Leo to come and get you in a few minutes and take you back to the house. I'll be here for long enough yet.'

'In the dark?'

'We'll rig up some torches.' He lifted his voice to hail the younger man who had just come into view around a far corner. 'Leo could do with a break. He's been down here since first thing yesterday morning.'

The other made no demur when given his orders. He looked pale with fatigue.

'You always seem to be catching me looking like something the cat dragged in,' he commented on a rueful note when they were in the Range Rover and heading away from the township.

'You can hardly expect to come through all that back there looking like something out of a bandbox,' she returned reasonably. 'Stop worrying about things that don't matter, Leo. Shall you be going back down there again tonight?'

'I must once I've had a couple of hours' sleep. There's a lot still to be done. Nick won't be prepared to leave off until things are shipshape again.' He turned the wheel to take the coming bend, and tagged on, 'How about calling in now for Nick's present? There couldn't be a better opportunity.'

Tara agreed halfheartedly. There was every chance Nick might not even be at home for his birthday if what Leo had said was true. 'I don't suppose any of you got much sleep last night,' she murmured, and he shook his head, with a wry little smile.

'Fitful dozing was the best I could manage. Lucky Nick started home when he did or he'd have been stuck for the night too once the big blow really got going. I calculated he would just about have reached the house by dark. Right?' He gave her a quick glance when she didn't answer. 'Aren't you feeling well? You look awfully pale.'

Shattered might be the best way to describe her feelings, Tara reflected numbly. If Nick hadn't been in Ruru throughout the night then there was only one other place he could have been: with Olivia. He had gone to her rather than come home.

'I'm fine,' she said, and wondered at the fact that her voice could sound so normal. 'Just a bit shaky, that's all.'

'Reaction, I expect. I think wind must be about the most frightening of the elements when it gets out of control. I remember one time . . .'

Tara was glad to let him talk. Anything was better than thinking. There didn't seem much damage to the bungalow when they finally reached it. She stayed in the car while Leo went to fetch the neatly wrapped package, taking it from him with fingers which felt nerveless.

'I'll have to pay you for it some other time,' she said as he got behind the wheel again. 'I don't suppose you'll want to hang around.'

'Oh, any time.' He was embarrassed again. 'Don't think about it.'

He took her right up to the house, shooting off again almost as she was out of the car. The lamps were already lit on the porch, glimmering out into the scented night. Anna came to greet her, her eyes following the vanishing tail lights with some surprise.

'Was that Leo? I'd have thought he'd be ready for a good meal.'

'He's more ready for a good sleep,' Tara said by way of explanation. 'Nick won't be back for some time yet, I imagine. He's determined to finish repairs in the town, at least.'

'He never could bear to leave things. He'll keep them at it till they all drop.' Anna cast a curious glance at the package in Tara's hands as they went indoors, but made no comment on it. 'You must be hungry yourself. Were things very bad at the clinic?'

'No, it was all very orderly. The doctor will be here by tomorrow, we hope, though I don't think he'll find all that much left to do.' She paused with her foot on the bottom stair. 'Where's Jenny?'

'In her room, I believe.' Anna looked faintly concerned. 'She's been unusually quiet all day. I hope she isn't sickening for something.'

If loving Nick was a sickness then it was already upon her, Tara thought with understanding and sympathy. Jenny's little world had fallen apart much as her own had done a short time ago. It was fairly apparent by now that she had indeed overheard her father's denial of her. Nothing else could have quelled her to such an extent. Tara wondered if she should go to her; but that could only make things worse. In Jenny's eyes she was the one who had precipitated this situation in the first place. The child was right too. She should never have married Nick. Life without him might have seemed bleak, but preferable surely to the kind of pain he inflicted on those closest to him.

The rain came while they were at dinner, soaking into the dry earth and releasing pungent odours of earth and growth to waft in through the open veranda doors.

'This will bring Nick home,' Anna commented with some satisfaction, viewing the downpour from the shelter of the veranda, coffee cup in hand. 'Even he can't keep things going while this lasts!'

She was proved right some half an hour later when they heard the sound of an engine turning into the drive. Slicking back damp hair, Nick came into the house, slacks and shirt dark with moisture.

'Another few hours and we'd have had it beaten,' he said in disgruntled tones. 'At least everybody has shelter for the night, even if it's only makeshift.' The eyes momentarily seeking Tara's were dull with fatigue. 'Don't look so tensed up. It's only weather. We don't normally suffer such extremes.'

'I know.' She made no attempt to add to the statement.

If the strain in her voice registered with him he didn't show it. 'I'll get into some dry clothes,' he said. 'You might get Liah to fix me a tray. Something cold will do. I'm not all that hungry.'

Tara avoided her mother-in-law's eyes as she moved towards the door leading through to the kitchen premises. Anna sensed something was wrong, but obviously could not be aware of the cause. Her request for food for the master was met with alacrity. On impulse she said she would take the tray up herself, though what she was going to say or do when she was alone with Nick she had no idea. Her own problems aside, there had to be something done about Jenny. One way or another Nick had to be made to see the truth.

He was standing at a window when she went into their room, wearing the thick white towelling robe which matched her own, his hair rough-dried and faintly curly at the ends. He turned as she crossed towards him, his eyes meeting hers with a look that seared.

'I opened the parcel,' he said, taking the tray from her to deposit it on the low table. 'Was it meant for me?'

'Not until tomorrow.' She was at a loss to account for the hardness in him. 'My own fault for not putting it away, but it doesn't really matter. If the rain stops I suppose you'll be going back to Ruru at daybreak anyway.' She paused, attempting the light touch. 'Perhaps I'd better wish you a happy birthday here and now.'

'With a present charmed out of another man?' His tone was heavy with irony. 'Sorry to put a spanner in the works, but that kind of dissembling is beyond me. First thing tomorrow Leo gets it back, along with a few choice words of my own!'

'Don't blame him.' Her voice was low and unhappy. 'I asked him for suggestions, Nick. I was desperate for something to give you, not having known beforehand. I . . .'

'You really think it means so much to me to have *presents* on the breakfast table?' The sarcasm grated. 'Oh, sure, if I hadn't happened to have seen that box among Leo's things when we moved him into the bungalow I might have appreciated the gesture—though I don't suppose it occurred to you that I might have wanted to know how you managed to get it through in time.' He paused there, eyeing her with something closely approaching dislike. 'How did you know about my birthday, anyway?'

'Jenny told me,' she said thickly. 'She was making you something special as a surprise.'

Dark brows contracted a little. 'Was?'

She shrugged, emotions locked away behind thin shutters. 'If she doesn't bother now you can hardly blame her. You're not her father, remember? You said so yourself. Perhaps it's a good thing in the long run. I doubt if you'd be capable of dissembling for her either.' Her control broke then, before the unrelenting coldness in the grey eyes, her voice suddenly impassioned as she added, 'How much longer are you going to go on blaming her for her mother's failings?'

'You don't know anything about it.' His tone was clipped and icy. 'Neither, if it comes to that, does *my* mother! And don't try denying she told you anything. That became pretty apparent the other afternoon.'

Tara felt sick. Nothing was going right. 'She was only trying to help,' she murmured, and saw his lips twist.

'Well, she didn't. Not knowing the facts, she couldn't very well.'

'The facts?'

'That's what I said. If you must have it in black and white, I have proof that Jenny isn't my child. Now will you leave it alone?'

'I can't.' She was shaken and dismayed. 'What kind of proof? She has your eyes, even some of your mannerisms. How *can* you go against things like that!'

'If you'd ever met her real father you wouldn't be asking.' A muscle jerked faintly in the side of his jaw as his teeth came together. 'We had other things in common besides Helen. And mannerisms, my sweet innocent, are acquired through imitation, not birth. I'm the only father she's ever known in person.'

'This proof.' Tara couldn't let it go; not now. 'It must be very conclusive to make you so certain.'

'It is.' The pause lasted mere seconds before he went on with some deliberation, 'Helen left me a letter the night she ran off with Ravel. I burnt it years ago, but I can remember it word for word. She told me Jenny was Paul's child; she could even name the occasion on which she was conceived. She said they were leaving her here on Mataleta because I could provide her with a better future. What she really meant was so that they could have a fresh start unhampered by a squalling brat. Satisfied?'

It was only the thought of Olivia that kept her from going to him then, from putting her arms about him and trying to blot out the memory of such pain. 'I'm sorry,' she whispered. 'Oh, Nick, I'm so sorry!'

His regard was bitter. 'Yes,' he said, 'so am I. I was a fool to imagine things might eventually work out. All I did in marrying you was to acquire another liability.'

'That's not fair.' She had gone white. 'I've tried to be ... everything you've asked of me.'

'And you think that's all there is to it?' He made a sudden impatient movement. 'You didn't understand one word of what I was saying the other night, did you? You're not

182

capable of understanding. Oh, I could train you right enough. I could make you mechanically perfect. Is that what you think I'm after?'

'No.' Her chin was lifted, her voice controlled despite the anger coursing through her. 'No, I daresay you'd only be satisfied to have me love you as much as Jenny does, because it's only then that you'd have the power to hurt the way *you* were hurt nine years ago. But it won't happen, Nick, because nothing can make me feel deeply about a man who uses people the way you do! So go on back to Olivia tonight too, if you like. At least from her you'll get the benefit of experience!'

He was staring at her as if he had never really seen her before. When he spoke it was in tones gone quiet and emotionless. 'Olivia left on the *Ballantyre* this morning. I put her on board myself after spending the night helping her pack her belongings and settling a price for the estate. I don't know where she's going, and I don't much care. Does that satisfy you?'

Shock held her rigid for a long, long moment. 'You mean you didn't ... want her any more?' she got out at last painfully.

'I haven't wanted her since the day I first met you,' he said with a flatness that was more convincing than any passionate denials. 'Before, yes. I left Mataleta because I wanted her badly enough to jeopardise my friendship with her husband. I'd lived for too long without a woman in close proximity, and she wasn't exactly discouraging. If John hadn't been so head over heels in love with her I'd have considered it a kindness to break the marriage up, because she certainly wasn't in love with him. She married him because he offered her a home and security without realising what life on a small island might be like for a woman used to leading a full social life. I was a way of relieving the boredom.'

'You were the reason she stayed as long as she did,' Tara said huskily. 'Without you she would have left John flat once she found out about his illness, and you couldn't let him go through that. While he was alive you had to keep her here, yet at the same time you couldn't betray him.' It all seemed so clear to her now, so perfectly, incredibly clear. Still not moving, she searched the lean features for some sign, but got nothing but an enigmatic regard in return. 'You . . . said you stopped wanting her the day you met me,' she appealed at length. 'I'm not sure what that's supposed to mean.'

'It means that I gained a new rather overriding interest.' The smile was faint. 'At first it was mostly that you reminded me of Helen at your age; especially in the way you came back at me. I wanted to put you down, make you smart a little; perhaps teach you what I failed to teach her. The *Saratoga* going down changed all our lives. You put your trust in me against all the odds; made me responsible for you. After that I couldn't let you go. I thought we had a basis to build on—not just physical need but emotional too. I wanted you to show yours for me in a deeper sense than just as a satisfactory lover and provider, but I'd to force you even into pretending by threatening to go to Olivia.'

'But you did go to her.' She still couldn't make herself believe what he seemed to be saying. 'You went to her last night in the middle of a gale.'

'Because she sent a boy through it in the car to fetch me, saying she'd had an accident. When I got there I found her right as rain but desperate for company. The weather worsened within a few minutes of my arrival. I was stuck there with her.' He paused and drew breath. 'I took the opportunity to say what had to be said—what should have been said that first night back when she coerced me into taking her home.'

184

Warmth was spreading through her slowly but surely, starting deep and uncurling into every part of her body. 'You realised that.'

'Of course. She wanted to talk about John, she said, about what his death meant to her. And she did talk about him too, in such a way I almost started to believe her feelings genuine. So I stayed—longer than I should have done. When I did get home you were fast asleep without a care in the world!'

'I wasn't.' Her voice was soft, her eyes misty. 'I'd been lying there imagining you with her and hurting like I'd never hurt before.'

She went to him then, half running, half walking into his arms, feeling them close about her, not merely in possession but in tenderness and understanding too. He didn't speak; there was no need. His lips said it all.

It took Anna's knock and her voice raised in urgent plea to break the spell. Nick was the first to move, going swiftly to open the door.

'Jenny's missing,' she said, face distraught. 'Her bed is empty and we've searched the house for her. Nick, if she's gone outside in this . . .' She left the rest of the sentence unsaid, her eyes going beyond him to Tara standing where he had left her. 'You know how oddly she's been acting all day.'

'Yes.' Tara jerked herself into action, closing her mind on the sudden fear. 'Nick, we've got to find her!'

'I know.' He was already half way across to the dressing room. 'I'll get some clothes on.'

He was back again inside a minute, still fastening the belt of his slacks. 'You looked everywhere indoors?' he queried as they descended the stairs together. 'No chance of her being inside?'

'Not unless she's found a hiding place we don't know about.' Anna could barely contain the worry in her voice.

'The veranda doors were open, and I'm sure we closed them when we came in just before you arrived. I've got Tamu out searching the grounds on the beach side.'

'Then I'll take the cliff path,' he said.

'*We'll* take the cliff path.' Tara was at his side, face pale but determined. 'You can't leave me out of this, Nick.'

He made no attempt to argue the point. 'Come on, then.'

They donned lightweight rainproofs before leaving the house, stepping down from the veranda into a night black as pitch and teeming water in one solid sheet. Tara could barely see a hand in front of her, but Nick seemed to know exactly where he was going, guiding her on across the grass by the light of the torch he carried and along the path they had taken together a few nights ago. It seemed so long ago now, like an episode from another lifetime. The misunderstandings were over, yet if they didn't find Jenny nothing would ever be completely right between them.

She could hear the sea as they approached the cliff, imagine the white foam of the waves breaking on the rocks below. In her mind's eye she saw the small body pulled hither and thither by the surging water, limp like a rag doll. When Nick stopped and caught her arm she could scarcely credit that the vague little shape squatting under a bush almost on the cliff edge was really alive.

'Don't startle her,' she whispered as Nick made to move again. 'Let me go.'

'No.' He was gentle but firm. 'I have to do this myself if it's going to be any good at all.' His hand pressed hers once, then let it go, but she had felt the tension in him. When he went forward towards the solitary little figure Tara stayed where she was, praying that his approach would be the right one.

'Jenny?' His voice was quiet but carrying even through the rain. 'What on earth are you doing out here in the wet?'

'Go away.' Her head had swung towards him, but she

made no attempt to get up. 'I'm not coming back with you. Ever! You don't want me.'

'Why don't I want you?' He had squatted close by the bush, though not close enough to touch her, the torch switched off now. 'Tell me, Jenny.'

'Because you've got Tara, and you love her instead of me.' It was the complete lack of emotion in the small voice that was the most distressing. 'You didn't even hear me calling you to come and look at what I'd found when we were at Taki Hill yesterday because you were talking to Tara.'

'That's true, I didn't. Perhaps your shout didn't carry far enough.' There was no hesitation as he went on, 'My loving Tara doesn't make any difference to the way I feel about you, honey. There are different kinds of love, that's all.'

This time the small, rain-plastered head turned the whole way towards him, although it was impossible to gauge her expression. 'Tara said that too once.'

'Because it's true.' Relief sent Tara forward without stumbling to sink to her knees on the soaked ground beside Nick. Jenny hadn't heard what he had said yesterday after all; she couldn't have done! 'Darling, we *both* want you! Very much. We always will. Let Daddy carry you home now before you get a chill. You don't want to be ill for his birthday, do you? What about your present?'

It seemed an age before the answer came. 'I threw it away. Over there.' At long last the deadness went from Jenny's voice, tears mingling with the rain on her cheeks. 'I made you a shell box for your cufflinks, like it said in my book,' she sobbed. 'And I've thrown it away. I'm sorry, Daddy.'

He handed the torch to Tara before reaching out to gather the child up in his arms, cradling the saturated little body to him. 'It doesn't matter,' he said. 'Honey, it doesn't matter! You can make me another. We'll look for the shells together, all of us. All right?'

The tears didn't stop, but the arm which crept up and around his neck was answer enough. He looked at Tara over her head. 'You'll have to lead the way back. Can you manage?'

'Yes, of course.' There was nothing at that moment that she wouldn't have done towards keeping that tenderness in his voice for them both. It wouldn't all be plain sailing from here, of course. Nine years of hurt would take a lot of eradicating, but she and Jenny would be equal to it. They were going to be a family at last.

Have you missed any of these best-selling Harlequin Romances?

By popular demand... to help complete your collection of Harlequin Romances

50 titles listed on the following pages...

Harlequin Reissues

Harlequin Reissues

Complete and mail this coupon today!